Bongwater

Bongwater

Michael Hornburg

Grove Press
New York

Copyright © 1995 by Michael Hornburg

This is a work of fiction. Any resemblance to actual persons, living or dead, is purely coincidental.

All rights reserved. No part of this book may be reproduced in any form or by any electronic or mechanical means, including information storage and retrieval systems, without permission in writing from the publisher, except by a reviewer, who may quote brief passages in a review. Any members of educational institutions wishing to photocopy part or all of the work for classroom use, or publishers who would like to obtain permission to include the work in an anthology, should send their inquiries to Grove/Atlantic, Inc., 841 Broadway, New York, NY 10003.

Published simultaneously in Canada
Printed in the United States of America

Library of Congress Cataloging-in-Publication Data

Hornburg, Michael.
    Bongwater / Michael Hornburg.
    ISBN 0-8021-3456-4 (pbk.)
    I. Title.
    PS3558.O6873B66   1995   813'.54—dc 20   94-39239

Design by Laura Hammond Hough

Grove Press
841 Broadway
New York, NY 10003

99 00 01 02   10 9 8 7 6 5 4 3

For Darcey with love

Gotta keep movin', can't stick around,
gotta get a ticket out of losers town.
—The Wipers

Bongwater

Part One

Portland

Jupiter faded as the first light spread over the western sky. Sitting on the roof, leaning against the brick chimney, I watched the sun creep over the Cascade Mountains. The sky changed channels from purple to gray and the bleary morning air smelled like worms.

I flicked the sparkling remains of my last cigarette between the buildings, just missing a fat green slug inching across the wet leaves plugging up the gutter, then climbed down the fire escape and crawled into the second-floor window.

Inside, empty beer bottles lined the hallway, the linoleum floor a sticky trail into the living room. Tony was passed out on the futon in the corner, mascara smeared over the cantles of his eyes, still wearing his lavender party dress, now hiked above his hairy knees. Robert crashed beside him, hogging the green comforter, snoring through his nose. The room smelled of beer and cigarette butts floating in the swill of plastic cups. The television was on, the sound muted, a test pattern stretched across the screen in black and white. Long blue shadows crept up the walls. The purple tulips were dying, their heads already drooping over the edge of the red bong.

I've been crashing here since the night a fire sent my apartment and all its belongings billowing into Heaven. I can still remember in minute detail how everything was arranged—the bookcase, my editing table, the drawings thumbtacked to the wall—how we picked through the rubble, found the melted records, the charred clothing. I'm still using the orange blanket the Red Cross gave me.

Robert and Tony rescued me after the fire, said I could stay with them until I found a new apartment. They're both queer as six fingers, but I've learned to love them just the same. They have an ambiguous relationship. I'm still not sure who is the transmitter and who is the satellite dish.

I went into the next room and sat on the dark brown couch, stared at the swirling patterns of the stucco ceiling, closed my eyes, the bright light of late-night caffeine quivering under my eyelids, my body simmering as the rush-hour traffic began its slow crescendo.

Robert and Tony's house is in Goose Hollow, a tiny

neighborhood sliced off from the city center by interstate highways at the foot of the West Hills. Because it's a hollow, the shade and rain keep it damp. Moss is growing on the front porch, the planks are soft with rot and sag. Last week I found a mushroom growing at the base of the bathtub.

It looked and smelled like any other squat, except Robert and Tony paid rent. Run down, but not too sleazy, the dark red carpeting in the front room was splattered with cigarette burns, a mismatched collection of dumpster furniture leaned against the scuffed-up walls. Most of the records were scratched, but that's the price you pay for roommates.

Starving, I decided to go downtown, get some coffee and a bite to eat. Looking around for my keys, I found a little bag of reefer on the floor, shoved it into my pocket for later. Sometimes it's best to be the last person at the party.

Up Jefferson Street, over the I-405 bridge, the wind picked up, my eyes got fuzzy, my fingers cold. I slid them into the front pockets of my jeans. Two men jogged past me in fluorescent Nike outfits marking their progress on digital wristwatches. Shopping-cart people were camped under the next bridge, their houses made of cardboard and plastic. Campfire smoke snaked up from the underpass.

I hurried over the windy bridge. *Robinhead* was playing at the Jefferson Theater. "She gave to the rich and she gave to the poor," the poster said. Mose Allison was doing a five-night stand at the Jazz Quarry. I've always hated jazz— boring solos and two-drink minimums.

Across the street was a Plaid Pantry. I went in and

bought a chocolate-frosted donut, then walked outside and spotted Jennifer at the Laundromat next door.

I once tried to be in love with Jennifer, but she wasn't very interested. Last month, after she got out of the hospital from one of her pill episodes, we drove down to Cannon Beach. On the way home she skidded off the road and crashed into a guardrail near the edge of a three-thousand-foot ravine. To prevent her from being recommitted, I told the police I was driving. Later that night she rewarded me with sex for the first and last time. After the fire I slept in her car for a week, but she never invited me upstairs.

Now we're just friends, I guess. She prefers men who seem preoccupied, who aren't totally smitten by her. Maybe it's the challenge or that she wants something difficult in her life. Her current infatuation with Robert makes perfect sense, someone who doesn't even like girls.

Sometimes her pharmaceutical accidents seemed like little dramas staged to end in brightly lit rooms, but when the voices in her head accelerated into visions, Jennifer had to go bye-bye.

When I visited her at the hospital, she was strapped down to her bed and I kind of think she liked it, as if she were dangerous or something. The all-new Jennifer has the same problems, different answers. Now I never know what to expect.

Wearing tight blue hip-hugger flares, a Vasarély T-shirt, and a thin black-leather choker with a blue stone, she looked like a charter member of the grungeoisie. Her cheeks flushed when she caught me staring like an imbecile, stuffing a donut into my face.

"Oh God, somebody call the police," she said, pushing her laundry into a large black duffel bag. The Laundromat smelled like a musty basement, an old woman sat beside the fogged window reading the *Oregonian* with a magnifying glass. My eyes clung to the colors spinning around in one of the dryers. Jennifer's laundry was almost all black.

"I like the little white ones best," I said, pointing at her underwear, stacked and folded.

"I'm sure you do, but they wouldn't fit you." Jennifer turned away to check her dryer, removed the last two socks.

"I don't wear underwear, I don't like the way everything gets all squished up in there. I gotta hang free."

"There's not much hanging from what I remember." She laughed, turned away, closed up her bags. "Be a good Boy Scout and help me carry these clothes back to my house."

"You got any coffee?" I asked.

"Sure."

"I want the other bag," I said. "The one with the panties in it."

"This one has panties, too," she said, handing me the heavy one.

We walked out of the Laundromat and up the hill toward Jennifer's place, across the Portland State campus, past the natural-food store jammed with hippies.

"I like your new haircut," I said. "You look like a boy."

"Gee, thanks."

"Where'd you get the tan?"

"I went skiing last weekend."

"With who?"

"With myself."

She seemed upset, edgy, the way all pill freaks are when their medication hasn't kicked in. Preoccupied, she acted as if I were a side effect from her multiple prescriptions. I shut up and followed her long legs up the hill. She was oddly hipless, like a skinny boy. Tall, with brown hair and blue eyes, she walked with nervous elegance, as if she were on a runway surrounded by cops.

Jennifer's apartment was in a converted hotel stuck between two Victorians, remnants from the old neighborhood destroyed when the federal government built the interstate. Portland is a cheap place to live, rents are low and there's no sales tax. However, most of the old wooden houses have no insulation. The apartment buildings with radiators are swarming with cockroaches, so you have a choice, freeze or bugs. Jennifer's place was sparse, a futon, some books, clothes piled neatly on metal shelves. Stark and angular, there was something Japanese about it, like a prison or a fashionable boutique. The emptiness always bothered me.

Jennifer unpacked her laundry bags, piling clean clothes onto the top shelves. I went over to her beatbox and sorted through the CDs: Aphex Twin, Orbital, Moby, and Nine Inch Nails. Jennifer worked at the UFO Cafe as "events coordinator," a fancy name for booking bands.

"Is techno still the rave at the UFO?"

"Techno and ecstasy," she said. "It's very sexy."

"All those hippies jumping around to disco? A bit scary, don't you think?"

"Maybe you should come down more often, a few nights in a smokey bar might do you some good. Maybe you'll get lucky and somebody will take you home."

Jennifer filled a small pan with tap water and placed it over an electric hot plate. I lay on the futon and stared at the sixty-watt bulb burning above her bed, then the little wind-up clock ticking away the afternoon. I could smell Jennifer in the white pillow, started to fantasize, watching her move around the apartment. The room was like a museum on a rainy day, bare white walls, high ceilings, polished wood floors. Jennifer was impossibly clean.

"Why don't you buy some furniture for this place?" I asked.

"I want to move to New York soon," she said, taking two cups from the cupboard. "I'm going tomorrow morning to check it out."

"You're going to New York?" I suddenly had an image of a bunch of bugs fornicating on a PBS special.

"It's getting to be so fucking boring here." She poured the boiling water through a Melitta filter.

"Why would New York be any different? You wouldn't even know anybody."

"I crave anonymity," she said. "And I do have a friend, Courtney, remember?" Jennifer turned away, poured milk into the coffee. "Besides, I'm worried about her, and you should be too."

Courtney was my roommate at the time of the fire. She disappeared that night and at first I assumed she was dead, but the investigators found no remains. A few days later she phoned Jennifer from Times Square, babbling on about some new rock star boyfriend. The fire had started in her room and it wouldn't surprise me if she had done it on purpose. She was always mapping out her disappointments in messy journals, but I never expected her to create such an intense drama. She really pissed me off.

"I'm sorry, I don't mean to be an asshole," I said. She handed me a cup of coffee. "I don't want you to leave." I grabbed her hand, forced her to look at me. "People who go to New York never come back the same."

"I don't want to be the same!" She pulled her hand away. "That's the point!" Jennifer went into the bathroom and slammed the door. I pulled out the Baggie I found at the house and started to roll a joint.

New York seemed like a huge festering wound, what was the attraction? We all read the same magazines, see the same films. Why does everyone insist on the New York experience? If you want to be surrounded by despair, move to North Portland. If you want energy, have a double espresso.

"Have you seen Robert today?" she asked from behind the door.

"Robert who?"

"Robert Robert, you know which Robert." The toilet flushed.

"You've got mirror balls for eyes, darling. Robert's on the futon with Tony this very minute."

"You are so wrong." She walked back into the room, stood by the window. "Robert may seem gay, but believe me, I know."

"Whatever."

"That's him! David, come here, look!" Jennifer pointed outside.

I set down my coffee and went to the window. Some old hippie was getting out of his Volkswagen van.

"See, I told you, every day the same thing."

"So what?"

"So, he's a psycho killer!"

"How can you tell?" I asked, watching him adjust one of his Birkenstocks.

"Just look at him." She pointed. "He's got a beard, a van, and he always carries those green garbage bags."

"Maybe it's his laundry."

Jennifer whirled around, paced across the room, a worried look crinkling her face. "This town is full of psycho killers!"

"He is definitely not a psycho killer," I said.

"How do you know?" She put her hands on her hips.

"Don't you watch television? Homicidal maniacs always look normal."

"Everyone in Portland fits that description!" she said, throwing her hands into the air.

"What you need is some protection." I pulled her belt loop, coaxing her closer to me, gave her the joint, then placed my arm around her waist.

"Stop it, you're giving me the creeps." She squirmed away, lit the joint with a small plastic lighter. Her pupils were dilated, her palms sweaty, and she had a peculiar body odor, eau de paranoia.

"You're so tense," I said as she picked tiny pieces of reefer from her little pink tongue. I rubbed her shoulders, her back muscles, following the outline of her bra.

"Cut it out!" she said.

"Why?"

"I have a boyfriend."

"You need a boyfriend."

"Robert is my boyfriend."

"Robert is your girlfriend."

"Fuck you." She got angry, pushed me away, walked across the room, and leaned against the bricked-up fireplace, the white mantel a landing for her immediate possessions: keys, a paperback of the *Basketball Diaries,* some unopened bills. She flipped through the envelopes. I followed her, stood behind her. She took another hit, then pressed out the joint in a silver ashtray. I put my arms around her. Jennifer turned around and pushed her hands against my chest.

"Stop it, please!"

"Give me a chance, I might start to grow on you."

"I don't want anything growing on me, thank you." She walked into the bathroom.

I turned away, stared out the window. The world outside was so perfect, all the cars parked between the painted lines. I wanted her in a bad way, but was so stoned everything had a doubling-over effect, this turned into that, and it was too risky to come to any conclusions, although my head was full of them.

"I have to take a bath and get ready for work," she said.

"Are you asking me to leave? What about the psycho killer?" I pleaded. Jennifer acted indifferent, handed me my flight jacket, kissed me on the cheek.

"It's better if you stand guard outside," she said. "Meet me at the UFO for a drink later, around eight, OK? I'll put you on the guest list." She pushed the door closed and I sauntered down the carpeted stairs imagining her sliding into a hot bubble bath, her naked white skin covered with goose bumps.

I crossed Alder Street headed toward Speed, a coffee-house downtown. The place was always crowded because the owner provided free newspapers and everyone was so cheap they'd go there just to save a quarter. The green door was propped open. I sat at a small table beside the radiator and ordered a breakfast special. The room was noisy, a K-tel compilation of seventies classics was blasting in the kitchen. The tiled floor reminded me of grade school, everything varnished and old, the mismatched tables and chairs the kind you see when someone clears out their basement and has a yard sale. Initials and names are carved into the wooden tabletops like picnic benches at interstate rest areas. Courtney used a penknife to carve her name into every single one.

Speed is a birthplace of conspiracy theories, a rest home for the terminally unemployed. For a single man, there's no better place to meet women, it's a neutral zone, like the library or a church.

Two girls in long flower dresses at the next table were gushing about some band that had played at the UFO the night before. The pretty one with short blond hair had gotten the drummer's phone number, the other was daring her to call right now. Her rosy cheeks flushed with embarrassment when she noticed me snooping on their conversation.

I stared at the wall opposite me. Band flyers were stapled over one another: Theatre of Sheep, The Vena Rays, The Miracle Workers, Candy 500. I should be in a band, musicians always get laid.

At the next table Simon was mesmerized by a Philip K. Dick paperback, his long thinning red hair noosed by a blue bandanna, like Dennis Hopper in *Easy Rider*, twenty years later. I heard him read last week at a UFO open mike. He rambled on about AIDS being a space virus brought back from the moon by homosexual astronauts, that the greatest failure of our generation was Hinckley missing his target, and that the hole in the ozone was in preparation for the second coming of Christ. A bad poet, but a good source of acid. There's a lot of sixties fallout living on the rim of Portland, like a cereal bowl the morning after, the milk gets hard and forms a crust impossible to scrub away.

Simon practically lives at Speed. He loves to tell stories about hanging out at Vortex with Hendrix, as if 1969 was last year, constantly reaching into flashbacks about his silver-glitter platforms, the methadone clinic, or the palm trees of Nam. He hates it when I make fun of his mellotron, some precursor to the synthesizer. Simon insists he was one of the original Paul Revere and the Raiders. Right.

I glanced out the window. A fat sparkling rainbow arched over the building across the street, a long line of people were waiting outside the record store, Dead tickets had just gone on sale.

Portland is a city of greens and grays, of wool sweaters and rubber shoes. The trees were ripening into autumn colors, the first winter rains had begun. There's a sense of dread this time of year, like running out of pot and knowing the only way to get high is to drink the bongwater.

The food came and I started shoveling it down, skimming the newspaper for atrocities, none of which really affected me anymore, just more inspiration to die in some spectacular fashion.

Rolling a cigarette, I added a little weed, turned through

the gray pages of the *Willamette Week,* nothing was hap-
pening. Jennifer was right, this town is deadsville. In the
Help Wanted section, someone had already circled counter
clerk at a video store. The paper listed a few other employ-
ment opportunities where the most challenging aspect of
the job was the psychological capacity to convince yourself
that you weren't a total loser.

"Anything else?" the waitress asked, scratching under
the collar of her black turtleneck. She added up my tab,
then set it between the salt and pepper shakers. I left a five
spot on the table, got up and walked outside, lit the cigarette, and headed back home to get some sleep.

At some point I hope to have a glorious alibi to cover up
the miserable failure of my life, like a car crash or brain
cancer. My greatest anxiety is that it won't come soon
enough. Passing the unemployment office, the line for food
stamps was curled around the room like rope stacked on a
sinking ship. I stopped at the Plaid Pantry, bought a lottery
ticket, scratched off the silver lining. Not even close.

New York

Courtney arrived at the flat and slammed the door. The doorway was slanted and the apartment drooped to one side. Old flowered wallpaper peeled away from the gray walls of the tiny kitchen. Three mismatched wood chairs surrounded a small Formica table. She tossed her jacket on the broken one and shook her dirty-blond hair, pulling it back into a ponytail, holding it in place with a rubber band from the collection wrapped around the bathroom door handle. She was wearing one baggy sweater over another, a white T-shirt poking out from under them like a skirt over her purple hip-hugger flares.

"Did anyone follow you here?" Tommy asked, eating a piece of white toast with green jelly spread across it. He wore a Sugarbuzz T-shirt with the sleeves cut off. MARY was tattooed in red letters across his pale skinny arm, below it in blue was LIED.

"Nobody followed me here, stupid. What are you eating?" She squinted.

"Toast."

"No, I mean, where'd you get the jelly?"

"In the fridge." He scratched his forehead, staring at the toaster.

Courtney opened the refrigerator, there was nothing inside. On the kitchen counter was a tube of generic mint gel toothpaste.

"God, you are so fucking gross," she yelled, looking back at him. Tommy was foaming at the mouth like a rabid dog, pouring sugar from little restaurant packs into a bottle of Pepsi.

"Why the fuck don't you snort the Sweet'n Low while you're at it!" She turned away.

"Did you hear that?" Tommy asked nervously. "I think there's somebody by the window." He pointed.

"Oh, shut up," she said, looking through the cupboards for something to eat. "If anyone's gonna kill you it's gonna be me!"

Tommy twitched, pushed his greasy black hair away from his eyes. Pimples dotted his forehead. He fingered the red shoelace hanging around his neck holding the two apartment keys, still staring at the window. Courtney let the tap run for a few seconds, then filled a glass with water, watched a baby cockroach squirm between the sink and the wall. The back window overlooked a dirty airwell, the ledge on the building next door was covered with bird shit, a fat black pigeon nested on top of it.

"Today, on my way to the subway, someone was watching me," Tommy said, chewing a mouthful of toast.

Courtney rolled her eyes, held the glass up to the light, then gulped down the cloudy water.

"When I turned the other way, someone else was watching. People were following me. Sometimes they would stop, look in a window or turn the corner, but another one replaced them, it was all perfectly synchronized."

"Maybe it was some of your fans." Courtney laughed.

The telephone rang.

"Don't answer it," Tommy screamed. They both lunged for the phone.

"Gimme that, asshole!" Courtney yelled. "I need a fucking job, Tommy!"

"Hello?" Courtney answered sweetly. "Hello?" The line was dead.

"See, I told you. They only call to see if we're here."

"Who, Tommy? Who?" Courtney slammed the receiver down and walked into the bathroom, sat on the toilet, just to be alone. Tommy warmed his hands over the glowing toaster.

"Never trust a telephone," he said. Courtney flushed the toilet, checked the zit growing on her chin in the mirror over the sink, noticed another one on her forehead.

"I'm goin' back out." She grabbed her jacket and slammed the front door. The hallway smelled like urine, the couple downstairs were yelling at each other in Spanish. Courtney thought about how much she hated New York. She'd been there maybe a month, but already felt the pollution seeping into her skin, sensed cancer growing. Pulling the front door open, she buried her face in the fuzzy lining of her jacket. Wind tipped over a garbage can, trash spilled onto the street. The can rolled away like a noisy tumbleweed. She found an old *People* magazine in the mess, tucked it under her arm, and walked over to Max Fish, sat at the swervy bar and ordered a happy-hour special, vodka and grapefruit juice. The pinball machine chimed in front, its blue siren light spinning around the room. She spread the magazine open, stared at the black and white photographs of celebrities. Someone tapped her shoulder. She turned and saw Bobby, a skatepunk she'd met last week at Tommy's Sunday matinee show at CBGB.

"What's up?" he asked. Bobby's baggy pants were scissored crookedly above his scuffed-up Doc Martens. He had on two thin jackets, his green hair was covered with a knit skullcap, three rings pierced his left nostril, a fourth one hung from his lower lip.

"I need a fucking job, a place to stay, how's that for starters?"

"Life sucks, don't it? What's up with Tommy? I thought you lived with him?" Bobby set his skateboard on the bar, it was covered with fading stickers.

"He's a fucking freak. He's afraid of the telephone, thinks he's constantly under surveillance."

"By who?" Bobby asked.

"How the fuck should I know?" she said. "He's a paranoid schizophrenic." Courtney sipped her drink through a tiny red straw.

"The perfect lead singer," he said, spinning the wheels of his board with the palm of his hand. "I thought you two were serious wango-tango?"

"We slept together once, but he was so drunk I doubt he even remembers," she said, crushing small ice cubes in the back of her mouth.

"You slept with him once and then moved in?" he asked.

"I needed a place to crash!" she said. "Fuck you, where do you stay?"

"At a squat on Ninth Street," he said.

"Oh, how glamorous," she mocked him, turning a page of the magazine, using her straw to make a wet spot between Madonna's legs.

"At least I have my own room," he replied.

Courtney was silent. The jukebox was booming, the bar had just been repainted Alice-in-Wonderland style. She identified with Alice, got soft for a minute, her shoulders drooped. She squeezed her lime over the melting ice cubes, thought about the smell of fresh-cut grass and swing sets, and the time she scraped her knee in the schoolyard after some little boy pushed her down.

"Tommy thought I had cameras behind my eyes," she said softly. "When I screamed he said it was feedback from my transmitter. He took a knife to my throat and asked who I was working for."

"Shit, he is crazy. C'mon, let's go get your stuff," Bobby
said. "You can move in with us." Bobby grabbed his skateboard. Courtney left two dollars on the bar and slid off her
stool. Outside, dust swirled in tiny tornados and a dog
wailed at a passing police car. Another police car sped past
in the opposite direction down Houston Street.

"Did you see that?" Courtney yelled. "Fucking cops
going in every direction. I swear, sometimes I think the city
pays them to drive around with their sirens on just to create
ambience for the tourists."

Bobby turned his head against the wind, hunched his
shoulders.

"It's fucking freezing out here. How far is it?"

"Around the corner."

They stopped in front of Tommy's apartment building at
Second Street and Avenue B.

"Let's just say we're doing my laundry." Courtney
rubbed her palms. "That way he won't suspect anything."
She pushed the steel door open and they walked up three
flights of stairs. The stairwell smelled of rotting garbage,
graffiti was scratched into the red steel doors.

"I'll grab everything and we'll make a run for it," Courtney whispered as she pushed her key in the slot and
opened the door. Tommy stood in the center of the room
wearing sunglasses, pointing a handgun toward the door.

"Who's there?" he yelled.

"It's Courtney, don't shoot!"

"Courtney who?"

"Courtney, you fuck."

He put the gun at his side, peered out the window, then

locked and chained the door behind them. Bobby sat down at the table.

"Who's he?"

"That's Bobby. He's an old friend of mine, he's gonna help me do the laundry," Courtney explained, then went into the bedroom and started stuffing her clothes into pillowcases, counting all the times she'd moved before, and then realized that every time she had fewer and fewer belongings. Tommy sat down across from Bobby, still holding the gun. Bobby stared at the map of the United States written in Arabic thumbtacked to the wall over the table.

"Sorry about the gun, but I have to take extra precautions this week. We're headlining at the Pyramid Club this weekend and I think the opening band tried to rub me out this morning."

"Really?" Bobby asked, scratching the stubble on his chin.

"I saw the assassin in the subway," Tommy said. "He wore a wireless speaker in his ear and was typing into a laptop computer. I got off the train immediately, but then realized it was only a ploy to get me into an unfamiliar location. The Canal Street station was deserted, an obvious hit."

Bobby turned away, trying to see what Courtney was doing. Courtney sorted through a pile of clothing on the bed. She noticed Bobby, rolled her eyes.

"So I leaned into an iron railing, knowing their heat sensors were probably already trailing me. I heard footsteps, but then they stopped." Tommy grabbed Bobby's hand and looked around the room suspiciously.

"Slow, precise," he whispered, "an agent, someone with cameras behind their eyes. And then a train roared into the station!" he yelled. "I jumped to the ground!" Tommy jumped onto the kitchen floor. "And fired several shots." Tommy shot the gun three times across the kitchen floor and into the stove.

"Jesus fucking Christ, Tommy!" Courtney yelled from the other room. Bobby covered his ears.

"I rolled onto the subway car and the doors closed behind me," Tommy continued. The neighbor pounded on the wall. "I got back here and helicopters have been circling ever since." Tommy stood beside the wall.

"Wow, that's wild," Bobby said, smiling. "Maybe that explains the Arabs parked downstairs."

"Where?" Tommy jumped to the window and pushed the shades open with the barrel of his gun. Courtney came into the kitchen.

"We're outta here," she said, relieved. "Give me ten dollars. No, fifteen. There's a lot of laundry." Tommy pulled out his wallet, gave Courtney a twenty.

"Here, take these, too." He handed her some tablets.

"What's that?" Bobby asked.

"Cyanide, in case you're captured. The torture could be gruesome."

"C'mon, Bobby." Courtney pulled his jacket.

"Thanks man," Bobby said and followed Courtney downstairs.

Outside the sky was a dismal yellow haze, the sun distant as the temperatures hovered in the forties. In front of the building, a couple of hooded Hispanic kids were pass-

ing a joint beside the bare bones of a stripped Ford, tiny
pieces of broken glass were scattered on the sidewalk.
"Bobby, where is this place?" Courtney asked. "Help
me carry something." Bobby took one of the plastic shopping bags.

"It's right over there." He pointed to a building with
windows of torn and shredded plastic billowing like flags.
Spray-painted slogans covered the stone face of the building, the sidewalk was missing.

"Did someone steal the fucking sidewalk?" she asked.

"I don't know, maybe."

"Are you sure this is OK?" Courtney stopped, looked
both ways.

"Yeah, c'mon." He shivered.

They crawled through an opening in the back of the
building. Busted cinder blocks, old clothing, and other trash
ringed the entrance.

"Bobby, wait up," she cried out, lugging her bags up the
splintered stairs. She turned down the corridor and saw
Bobby waiting in a doorway.

"Here we are," he said.

"Where? Where are we, Bobby? This is it?" she asked.
Courtney looked around in disbelief. Newspapers were
pasted onto the walls for insulation and plastic was stapled
over it. There was a futon in one corner, covered with a
sleeping bag. A WIGSTOCK poster hung on one wall and a COP
SHOOT COP on the other, there wasn't any other furniture.

"This used to be a hotel," he said, pushing some paper-
backs off the futon.

"Used to," Courtney repeated. "What's that smell?"

"What smell?" he asked. "You sleep there." He pointed.

"Where do you sleep?" she asked.

"I sleep there, too."

"Uh-uh, no way, Bobby, I don't sleep with strangers."

"You slept with Tommy, there's nobody stranger than him. Besides, I rescued you, I'm the superhero."

"Yeah, and this is the Honeycomb Hideout," she snapped. "Is there a phone? I need to make a call."

"Sure, it's around the corner."

"This one?" She pointed at the doorway.

"In front of the bodega on Fourth and C." He pointed. "That way."

Courtney turned and stomped down the stairs. She walked outside, spotted the phone booth, ran to the corner, and picked up the receiver, but the phone was dead, all the push buttons had been smashed.

"Hello?" she said softly. The receiver fell from her hand. A little Hispanic man approached her.

"Hey lady, you want to make some money?"

Portland

It was almost ten, so I walked downtown to meet Jennifer at the UFO Cafe. A large black flag hung over the entrance, some band from Seattle was unloading amplifiers from their van. I pulled the silver door open, went inside. The room was lit with black lights in satellite fixtures, red balls surrounded by purple neon rings. Fluorescent psychedelic patterns spread over the walls, blue Astroturf covered the floor. The long silver bar was actually the wing of an old World War II fighter plane, shot down, legend has it, by a UFO.

Ambient techno blasted from the P.A. speakers in the backroom, a mirror ball kept a blizzard of light swirling over the
dance floor.

I found a small round table against the wall and settled
in. It was early, but the bar was already packed with regulars, most of them notorious for slam dancing with sister
midnight.

Sheila was flirting with some women at the far end of
the bar. She waved her beer at me. I waved back. She was
a sloppy blonde, in dirty jeans and small John Lennon
glasses, an artist and filmmaker who'd turned to pornogra-
phy to pay the bills. She'd been bugging me since the fire to
show up at one of her shoots. The cash would be useful, but
it'd be a long jones in hell before I'd flash my ass for a fix.
She says her porno is political. Whatever.

"What happened to you this morning?" Sheila yelled.

"Herpes flared up." I acted disappointed. She
scrunched her nose, turned her back to me, whispering into
the ear of the tall skinny blonde with the swollen eyes and
a red dragon tattoo slithering up her arm.

An SRL video flashed across the TV monitor above the
mirrors lining the back wall. There was a twelve-foot shock-
wave cannon and a car with square wheels, the crowd
cheered whenever something exploded.

Jennifer sat down beside me, dressed in one of her solid
black uniforms, little pieces of white lint glowing under the
black light.

"I have this idea for a new film," I said.

"I thought you were supposed to be in Sheila's film
today?" She waved at Sheila.

"Oh that, her movies have only two plots, in and out. The film I want to make would star you and me."

"Oh really?" she seemed slightly interested, watching the band move their equipment in. "How many plots does your film have?"

"I would be the Minister of Disco and you would be the Ambassador of Love—crazed youth fighting international crime in a red Italian sports car."

"Sounds like Mod Squad to me," she said, unimpressed.

I looked up and saw Lisa leaving with the guitar player, probably walking him out to the van for a blow job. Lisa uses men like matches. I slept with her once, but so has nearly everyone else in Portland.

"C'mon, let's go dance a little bit." I tried pulling Jennifer away from the table.

"OK," she said, "but not here." She led me to the front door then veered off into the bathroom. "Wait outside."

I went out the door, lit a cigarette, and leaned on the band's van. The meter was expired, I put a nickel in, bought some time. Lisa hates to be interrupted. Two hookers leaned against the brick wall of the UFO, wobbling in their platform shoes.

"How 'bout a slow ride?" The taller one winked at me.

Jennifer came through the door swinging her black leather bag over her shoulder. I followed her down Sixth Street.

"I'll do ya better than them chicken legs," the hooker yelled out.

"Friends of yours?" Jennifer asked.

"Relatives," I said.

She stopped, opened her bag, took out her cigarettes. I looked back up the street, the hooker waved at me, a street-sweeper whisked the curb opposite.

"Hey Jennifer, when you were in high school, were you a cheerleader or a pom-pom girl?" I asked as we turned the corner onto Couch Street.

"Why?" She seemed irritated.

"Well, pom-pom girls practice precision, which is the quality you have on the outside, and cheerleaders stomp their foot and scream a lot, which is the quality you have on the inside."

"And your conclusion?" she asked, stopping to light her cigarette.

"Neither, I guess, too cool for that shit, right?"

"Right."

We went into the Wild West on Broadway, a disco jammed with one hundred men in skintight jeans. It's the oldest bar in Portland, been here since the first trading post, there are still bullet holes in the woodwork. I heard Lewis and Clark drank here and that Patsy Cline once made a surprise visit. These days the biggest celebrity you'll see is some tired old drag queen from New York. The room was extremely hot, it smelled like a gymnasium. I looked around and counted moustaches.

"C'mon." Jennifer pulled me. Light swam between the sweaty bodies, the bogus scent of cheap perfume and locker-room funk hung in the air, the new Boy George single came on, Jennifer handed me some rush.

"What's a raging disco without poppers?" I asked, taking a hit. "Saving the good stuff for later?" I handed the tiny brown bottle back to her, we danced at one end of the floor. Jennifer was scanning the crowd, her body moving unconsciously, her tummy making slow circles, her Saturn medallion bouncing off her chest. I placed my hands over the back pockets of her jeans, she pushed me away, annoyed. This was a losing situation, I was wasting my time. She was here to find Robert, I was just a prop.

"You want a drink?" I yelled over the music.

She nodded and I spun off to the bar, pushed between four sailors, ordered two beers. Some guy with a gray moustache and tight black leather pants started hitting on me, offered me some quaaludes. I ignored him, stared at the wagon wheel over the bar and the autographed picture of Divine beside the totem pole. When I looked back over the dance floor, Jennifer was passing through the crowd in the direction of Robert's table. I left the beers with two Black drag queens in matching silver dresses and walked out the door.

It was raining, it's always fucking raining in Portland, clouds hang over the city like heavy drapery. I stood under the Broadway Hotel awning contemplating where to go next. A pair of shopping-cart people were curled into sleeping bags, leaning against the boarded-up doors, sharing a bottle of Thunderbird, listening to the Blazers game on a transistor radio.

I ran into the rain, headed back home, when I remembered the party Robert told me about at the Myler Building above Habromania. A group of clothing designers were doing a stupid theme party: beatniks, jug wine, some bongos, a six-pack of Karl Marx.

Dashing across Burnside, I jumped over puddles, but

my shoes and socks were soaking wet before I reached the end of the block. A locomotive pushed a carload of grain toward the Blitz-Weinhard Brewery, a thick yeasty scent spread over the neighborhood. Behind the telephone building, a single red bulb lit the entrance. The door was open, so I walked up the tiled staircase.

"If it isn't stranger danger," a voice called out.

I looked up. "Hi Mary," I said, wiping my feet.

She placed a string of black and red beads around my neck from a pile on the counter, then kissed me on both cheeks.

"You're soaking wet, let me have your jacket."

I unbuttoned my jacket, handed it to her. She wrapped it around the banister.

Mary was wearing a little green miniskirt and white kneesocks. She reminded me of a Girl Scout in a porno movie. She was thin and long-waisted, and her black hair was parted in the middle and curled down to her shoulders. She wore a silver necklace with an Indian emblem, a white T-shirt with a black suede vest.

"You want a glass of red wine?"

"Sure." I followed her down the narrow hallway.

Everybody looked rather stoned, the sweet smell of hash calmed my stomach. The hallway was filled with young boys sporting perfect haircuts, I felt as if I'd just gone through a revolving door.

"So what's new?" Mary asked.

"Oh, you know, me and Jack are thinking of taking the Pontiac down to Mexico," I said. "Maybe write some poems."

"Very funny," she said, leading me into another room.

"We've all got something we want to run from, I've been running all my life, and, to tell you the truth, I'm tired of it." Mary poured red wine from a large green jug, passed the cup over to me, brushed her hair away from her face.

"What about you, David? What are you running from?" She touched a button on my flannel shirt, sipped her wine. I thought about the answer, but wasn't sure how to fill the awkward silence, took a sip of wine, shrugged my shoulders.

"You can tell me later." She winked and led me into another room. "C'mon, I'll introduce you to everyone."

"Oh God, no . . . please, not acoustic guitars," I said.

"They won't hurt you."

"Yes, please, I'm allergic. I'll get a rash. Can't we go over in the next room, you know, chill out a bit?"

She led me into the backroom of the building and we sat alone on top of cardboard boxes beside a large window. The neon outside made the rain-slick street kaleidoscopic.

"Is this where you work?"

Mary nodded. "A bit messy, huh?" Mary's workroom had hundreds of photographs torn out of magazines taped to the walls. Rolls of colorful fabric leaned against the wall, millions of little pieces were strewn across the floor. A naked mannequin leaned against the far wall, one arm missing.

"Where do you work?" she asked.

"I'm in between jobs at the moment, so what's with this party?"

"We just finished a new line, a seventies groupie look."

"Why is everyone suddenly so in love with the seventies?" I asked.

"It's the recession, really, people are trawling thrift stores, the tackier the better, it's a backlash against good taste. The seventies had the coolest music, disco and punk. I don't know, it's a trend, what can I say?"

"What will come next?"

"Well," she paused, "it definitely won't be an eighties flashback. The millennium countdown will probably kick in soon, everything will get very gothic and weird, mix in a little end-of-the-century-new-age glam and presto, instant zeitgeist. You want some more wine?"

"Sure." I held out my glass. Mary filled it, pulled a joint from her vest pocket.

"You got a light?" she asked.

I took the matches out of my back jeans pocket, lit the end of her joint, the flame shadowed the soft circles under her pale blue eyes. We took a few hits in silence, watching rain pour onto the empty sidewalk. A police car cruised Stark Street, its searchlight peering into shopwindows. Mary blew a thin tendril of smoke against the glass which curled back in waves, then drifted toward the ceiling.

"I'm sorry about your house burning down, Robert told me all about it. Did you really lose everything?"

"Yep."

"What a drag, that would kill me," she said.

"Nothing was left anyway, Courtney smashed all the good dishes during one of her tantrums, the carpeting was painted red in the midst of a fierce acid binge, the walls covered in crayon drawings. In some ways, it was more Courtney's place than mine."

"How did it happen?" she asked.

"I don't know."

I remembered Courtney's room, lit by candles, choked with incense and cigarette smoke, thought about the flames leaping out of the windows, the dry summer wood burning like kindling, the fire trucks pouring water on the houses next door, letting ours burn to the ground.

"So what are you gonna do now?" She passed the joint over to me.

"Well, once I get a new place and a little more settled down, I want to start a new film about two superheroes called the Minister of Disco and the Ambassador of Love." I took a hit. "They battle the criminal nature of mankind, two lost souls looking for love in a red Italian sports car."

"I thought you were the criminal nature," she said, taking back the joint.

"I've been doing time at the library, whirling through microfiche, gathering info on a pair of millennialists called Him and Her, a unisex cult group based in Oregon in the seventies. They promised their followers a spaceship was coming to pick up the chosen. The privileged proved themselves by giving up their earthly belongings."

"Wow, that's weird, I think my parents were into that," she said. "When they gave up the old Ford, Him and Her said the spacemen would prefer the BMW. Dad got kind of suspicious." She took back the joint.

"I'm looking for a leading lady," I said.

"That's what Robert says." She turned away, relit the joint, her cheeks blushing like little pink clouds. "I heard you're gonna be in Sheila's new movie, now there's something I might be interested in." She laughed, handed me the roach.

"I overslept and blew my chance at stardom."

"Too bad," she said, "for Sheila I mean." She reached over her pattern tables, pushed the play button on her boom box. I caught a glimpse of a little rose tattoo on her upper thigh, felt an erection press inside my jeans. *Exile in Guyville* warbled from the tiny speakers.

"So where did you grow up?" she asked. "You're not from Portland."

"Downers Grove," I said.

She started laughing, choking on her wine. "What?"

"Downers Grove," I repeated. "It's a suburb of Chicago."

"Sounds depressing."

"I spent a lot of time riding around in the backseat of friends' cars, circling cul-de-sacs in search of parties. I remember looking out the window thinking, at least I'm moving forward."

"Is that how you got here?" Mary laughed.

"Sorta."

"You have brothers or sisters?"

"A sister. She's a bartender in New Orleans, has tattoos all over her body. She's gone completely mad."

"Wow, I'd like to meet her."

"What about you?" I asked.

"I've been in Portland all my life, went to MLC, Lincoln High, and Reed College."

"What did you study at Reed?"

"Sex and death."

"In that order?"

"They're requirements at Reed." She crossed her legs.

"Did your parents join the cult?"

"They both became psychologists. They work the touchy-feely make-everybody-happy trail. It's a scam, but what isn't. Everybody's looking for something to fill up on."

Mary walked over and pulled my hand. "You want to dance?" she asked.

"Do I have a choice?"

"Nope." She leaned her head against my chest while Liz sang her Canary song. I could feel the quick pulse in her wrist, her hair smelled like smoke. We swayed slowly in the room, then, drunkenly, she leaned into me. I felt embarrassed about my erection, tried to lean away, but Mary pressed against me.

"Are you still involved with Jennifer?" she asked.

"She's just a friend. Jennifer has a crush on Robert."

"Robert is a fag." She stopped dancing.

"You know, I know, every queen in town knows, everyone but the princess herself."

"That girl needs to have her gaydar checked." She leaned her head against my shoulder, started dancing again.

"What about you? Who's your man?" I asked, resting my hand on her hip, rubbing the side of her leg.

She leaned into me, looked up toward the ceiling.

"Let me see your palm," she said, swaying slightly. I extended my hand and she held my fingers, tracing the crosshatchings in my palm. She pointed.

"Here is your life line and here is your love line." Mary rolled up my shirtsleeve, slid her fingers up and down the soft underside of my arm. "You have great veins."

The wind picked up, rattling the windows, the rain falling even harder. Mary let go of my hand, walked across the room, and opened the far windows.

"I love the sound of rain," she said.

A cool gust of wind cut across the workspace, loose paper and materials scattered in the breeze, the room glowing in the soft blue haze of streetlight.

Mary was several years younger than me, but surrounded herself with older men from the theater crowd, looking for work, I guess, doing costume design. She was good-looking in a flower-power way. Very calm, very much in control, she seemed to be making all the first moves. I felt drawn to her lingering eyes, aroused by her lazy body language, suddenly lusting for her hot little bod. I stood beside one of the worktables.

"How about whipping something up for me real quick?" I asked, playing with the controls of a sewing machine.

"I never operate machinery under the influence of alcohol, there's a warning sticker." Mary walked back toward me.

"Since when do you heed warnings?" I asked.

"I'm a very cautious person." Mary sat on the floor, leaned against a file cabinet, made a little box with her hands in front of her eye.

"What are you doing?" I asked.

"I want to see what you'd look like in a porno movie." I took a step away from the radiator.

"No, stay right there. The lighting is perfect." Mary tilted farther toward the floor. I stepped over her, sat down beside her. She put her arm over my shoulder and pressed her lips onto mine.

New York

Walking back to the squat, Courtney had trouble negotiating the broken sidewalk. The East Village was not designed for platform shoes. The little Hispanic man followed her back to the building, repeating himself, in a thick Puerto Rican accent.

"C'mon lady, I take you for a ride in a taxi. We go to my brother's house in Queens. You like it there, not like here, you know. He has two telephones!"

"Fuck off." Courtney passed through the back-lot doorway and headed up the dirty gray stairs.

Bobby was lying on the futon, his shoes off, writing in a journal. Two fat candles burned in a black skillet beside the bed giving the room a sullen amber glow.

"I'm sorry, Bobby, I didn't mean it." Courtney crawled onto the futon and lay on her stomach beside Bobby and closed her eyes.

"You gonna take off your shoes?" Bobby asked.

"Nope," she said.

Bobby leaned over and blew out the candles, then curled up beside her. The room was suddenly black, Courtney pulled the big blue sleeping bag up to her shoulders. She could hear people shouting upstairs, outside a car alarm screamed. She rolled over, turned her back to Bobby, shivered.

"Are you asleep?" she asked.

"No."

"Good, don't go to sleep before me or else I'll get scared."

"There's nothing to be scared about, I promise," he said.

"How do you get the space heater to work?"

"The streetlight out front is wired."

"Is that safe? I mean, we won't die in a fire or something?"

"At least it'll be warm." He rolled over, pulled the sleeping bag closer to his chin.

"Do you pray before you go to sleep?" she asked.

"No. Never. Do you?"

"No." She brushed her face against the coverless pillow.

"Do you think Jesus was a homosexual?" she asked.

"Where'd you get that idea?"

"Well, you know, he hung out with all those guys."

"The twelve disciples," he said.

"Yeah, so he cruises the desert with twelve guys, but never sleeps with anyone, I'm sure."

"Maybe he takes after his mother. What's your point?"

"It's a big cover-up! I mean, what if fags were holy or something, the world would be so much different."

"Maybe Jesus was really ugly or had b.o.," Bobby said.

Courtney pushed his hand off her thigh. Bobby was nice, he just needed a shower, like, three days ago. And there was no way she could have sex in a building without doors. She stared into the darkness, the room seemed more pleasant when you couldn't see it. It was just a room, a place to sleep. Her eyes focused on a thin strip of orange streetlight bleeding past the edge of cardboard tacked over the window.

Bobby's cold hand reached over her arm onto her stomach, then crept toward her breast. She grabbed his hand, pushed it back.

"Not tonight," she said. "I'm on the rag, leave me alone or I'll do a Carrie number all over your futon."

Bobby was silent, pretended he was asleep. Courtney lay in the dark, her eyes open, the sweet smell of candle smoke filling her head, wondering about tomorrow and the day after that. She promised herself that all this was temporary, that all this was necessary.

"Bobby?"

"What?"

"Are you asleep?"

"No."

"What were you writing in your journal?"

"Stuff."

"Is it about me?"

"No."

"Oh." She sounded disappointed. "Do you want to be a writer someday?" She sat up, unable to get comfortable on the futon.

"Maybe," he said.

"I think you should reconsider." She stared at the doorway.

"Why?"

"Nobody reads anymore, you have to think visual, something that people can react to."

"Like a billboard?" Bobby mumbled.

"Very funny. Who's more popular, Samuel Beckett or Vanna White?"

Bobby didn't answer.

"You see, and they both work with words."

Portland

I left Mary's late that night. As I headed back home, the air was so clear the skyscrapers sparkled like Oz. Seagulls floated over Sixth Street, white wings against a black sky. A queasy electric feeling rippled inside my stomach. Mary's taste still in my mouth, her ghost like a second skin. The streets were empty and the city had that eerie *Omega Man* feeling, like I was the last man on Earth. Mary was great, but something creeped me out about her. She reminded me of Beth, my lab partner in high school. They shared the same cynical smile, as if nothing I said would ever surprise them. They both wore a lot of rings, had the same color hair, and the same thick scars on the underside of their wrists. One day Beth got into a stranger's van outside the Meadowbrook Mall arcade and was found a month later hacked to pieces in a Hefty garbage bag.

A chill spread through me as the Tri-Met bus came squealing to a stop. I jumped on and sat toward the back, swarmed by high school memories.

Graduation night, I went to see Black Sabbath with two friends, Gary and Phil, at the International Amphitheater, a cow showroom on the South Side of Chicago. We were wasted on angel dust and had got our hands on some whiskey in the city. On the way home, Gary drove wildly down I-55, swerving across all four lanes.

In Downers Grove, two hundred and fifty new houses were going up on an old farm between Sixty-third and Seventy-fifth Streets. The cornfields surrounding my school were being plowed into cul-de-sacs. Blacktop was spreading like cancer. Shopping malls, chain stores, and fast-food restaurants appeared overnight. Gary drove around a barricade and into the development, speeding along the curving dirt roads that sliced through a field of waist-high weeds blinking with fireflies. Half-assembled houseframes stood open and vacant, stacks of two-by-fours, roofing material, and bags of cement in the driveways.

Gary would never admit it, but he feared the end of high school. None of us had jobs, none of us was going to college. He hated how everything was changing, as if something were being taken away by someone he didn't know.

He was in a typical Saturday-night frenzy, had already slammed a six-pack of Old Style, and had that shit-eating grin on his face like he was eager for trouble. He would usually take out his frustration on inanimate objects—mailboxes were a favorite target. Heavy machinery was parked alongside the roads, bulldozers and Caterpillars. Gary wanted to hot-wire one, take it for a joyride, knock over a lightpole.

Lifting his handgun from under the vinyl bucket seat, Gary started shooting at the empty houses while doing donuts on the unpaved cul-de-sac. A huge cloud of dust swallowed the streetlight, the car tilting like it might tip over. He stopped in the circle and aimed for some windows, shattering one on his third shot. Phil and I were cheering him on, all three of us dusted out of our minds. A police car swerved onto the cul-de-sac, a voice shouting over a loudspeaker. I couldn't hear what he said, the music was cranked, Jimmy Page wailing. Gary put the car in gear and drove straight at them, trying to get away.

Phil braced himself against the dashboard. I ducked behind the seat, expecting a crash. Gary sped up, stuck his gun out the window, and fired at the cops. Bullets came crashing through the windshield, shattering the glass, striking Gary on the left side of his head. The car went out of control, spun wildly, jumped the curb, and sailed through the weeds into the open foundation of a new house. The music was still blasting, I crawled up from the backseat. Bright red blood gushed from Gary's ears, nose, and mouth, oozing into a puddle already forming in his lap. Phil was screaming, blood splattered his face and jeans. I leaned up

and turned off the engine, unbuttoned my jean jacket,
threw it over Gary's face. Phil pushed open the mangled
door, a high-pitched squeal of bent steel echoed across the
field.

The cops were squatting in the weeds at the edge of the
house foundation, guns drawn, their flashlight beams peering into the car window.

Phil got out first. I pushed up the bucket seat and followed. The tall one grabbed my hair and slammed my head
against the hood. In the windshield I saw Gary's blood
soaking into my jean jacket. The other cop shoved Phil
down beside me. We were frisked, handcuffed, read our
rights, then pushed into the backseat of a police car. Several
more police cars arrived, followed by two ambulances and
some fire trucks, red lights swept across the field.

Driving to the police station, Phil bent over, hung his
head between his knees. I could hear him quietly sobbing.
I stared out the window, saw the flashing yellow streetlights
on Main Street, the boarded-up Sears store.

Gary's mother insisted on an open casket. It took some
nerve to enter the funeral parlor, an old gothic building on
the north side of town stuffed with antiques.

His coffin was a tin box airbrushed a pale red and gray
like an Econoline van. Silver ornaments embellished the
corners, the way pimps decorate Cadillacs. Surrounded by
fan-shaped flower arrangements, Gary looked plastic, like
something in a wax museum. His skin was swollen and his
eyes sewn shut, his hair greasy and combed forward, parted
in a way he never wore it, his forehead pieced together with
clear plastic thread. He was wearing the blue polyester suit

he wore to the prom. Staring into the casket, I half expected him to smile, this being another one of his elaborate practical jokes.

A week later, Phil coaxed me out to a party. All my friends were getting fucked-up at some girl's house, her parents were out of town. Nobody had much to say. Gary's girlfriend was making out with some jerk she'd met at a kegger the night before in Westmont. His older brother got so drunk he fell through the sliding screen door. Phil and I started talking about a road trip, not just Wisconsin, something big. Two days later we packed and drove straight west to see the Pacific Ocean.

The car broke down in Portland, a piston blew and the cylinder cracked. The gas-station mechanic bought the remains for seventy-five dollars. I rented a studio apartment on Twenty-first and Northwest Hoyt and found work soon after on an assembly line making window blinds. The new job was therapeutic in its monotony. It settled me down. Phil left after three months to join a fire crew in southern Oregon. He's been down there ever since, growing weed.

I spent a lot of time wasting time, high on ecstasy, chasing the little white dots of mirror balls in the City Club or Metropolis. From one empty glass to another, sleeping with strangers, my life seemed pointless. My only friends were the assholes at the blind factory.

One night, I watched a crew shoot a low-budget film in a transient bar in Old Town, a story about a grocery clerk in love with a young Mexican boy. The slow process drew my attention. I started going to double features every weekend at Cinema 21, watching films for camera angles and flaws in continuity. One weekend I bought a Super-8 camera and a projector at a pawn shop on Second Street and started making my own films. First, single-frame three-minute cartridges, short collages of speed and color, then longer narrative pieces about conspiracy theories. I entered one in the West Coast Film Festival, won a scholarship at the Museum Art School, was given access to sixteen-millimeter equipment, and made a seven-minute color film from a surrealist play. The more ambitious the project, the more difficult it became. Film is an expensive medium. All my editing was done on dual wind-up reels and a funky lightbox I found at a garage sale, the only decent actors were Robert's drag queen friends.

I was academically backward, never finished the projects on time, argued with my instructors, was given "Incompletes," and eventually thrown out of the program. When the film was finished, I showed it at the UFO Cafe, there wasn't any other venue. It was never shown again, then destroyed when my house burned down.

The bus stopped downtown in the mall, I got out and walked the rest of the way. It was a starless night, silent white satellites circled invisible overhead, fog thick as a hangover hung over the city. As I got closer to the house, music became audible, a block away I could already recognize the songs. Our building was lit up, some guys were out on the fire escape.

"Who are all these people?" I asked Robert, wiping my shoes on the living room rug.

"Tabloid wanna-be's," he slurred.

There were some musicians I recognized. A few lonely fag hags clung to a circle of pretty boys, constantly glancing over their shoulders, looking to see who was looking.

Robert was wearing a blue shark-skin suit, his tie was missing. He was holding the remains of a martini, swaying in blissful intoxication. It was 6:00 A.M. and the party was winding down, the few last ecstasy whores dancing through the room.

"Sometimes I feel like a port in an ocean of human waste," Robert said, toasting the crowd, his eyes blinking slowly.

"How poetic," I said. "I'm going upstairs to crash."

"With this noise?" he asked.

"Not even you could keep me awake." I winked.

"You're such a tease."

I went up to my room and opened the door. Tony was kneeling on my mattress, panty hose pulled down to his knees, his baby blue dress lifted and a naked boy devouring his cock. White light from the hallway spread over them.

"Out!" I yelled.

The naked boy jumped up, blushing nervously, picked up his clothes, and hurried past me. Tony acted put out, pulled up his nylons, and left the room.

"Party pooper," he said in passing.

The phone started ringing, but nobody bothered to pick it up, or nobody could hear it over the music. The party was into its second shift, people who work at night, the cocaine crowd. I picked up the extension at the top of the stairs.

"Hello?" I shouted, putting a finger in my other ear.

"Why'd you ditch me?" It was Jennifer, I had forgotten all about her.

"You seemed to be in good hands," I said.

"He's a dreamboat, isn't he?"

"Where are you?" I asked.

"At the airport, I'm going to New York, remember?"

"Oh yeah."

"Where'd you go?" she asked. "You weren't at home when Robert and I got there."

"I crashed Mary's party."

"You may as well have gone to a whorehouse."

"Like the Wild West is a church."

"The Wild West is a sanctuary of sorts," she said. "So, is Mary still a topless dancer—I mean, a clothes designer?"

"You're cheap, Jenny." I looked down the stairs but didn't recognize a soul, more dudes with brand new haircuts. A heavy cloud of desperation hung over the room. Tony was orbiting, refilling glasses with straight shots of vodka, his free hand making wild dramatic gestures with a foot-long cigarette holder, trying to seduce a freshman from Reed parked on the couch.

"Mary's a little young, don't you think?" she asked.

"A little young for what?"

"She's a budding nymphomaniac, the Anaïs Nin of the Sassy generation. I hope you got laid." She acted indifferent. "She'll just use you. She uses everybody."

"I want to be used, why should you care?"

"I care about you, David, don't you care about me?"

"You shouldn't go to New York," I said. "It's gonna fill your head with crazy ideas."

"What are you afraid of, the crazy or the ideas?" she asked.

"The crazy, Courtney's a loose end, you shouldn't attach yourself."

"Just because she burnt down your house is no reason to hold a grudge," she said.

"I lost everything in that fire!"

"So did Courtney."

"Courtney didn't have anything!"

"You're such a materialist. Who cares about a bunch of dumb old junk anyway? Junk is junk, go out and buy some new junk."

"Listen, I gotta go," I said.

"Is Robert there?" she asked.

I slammed down the phone, went to pee before crashing. Robert was in the bathroom shaving his chest hairs. An inch taller than me, with broad shoulders and fierce cheekbones, he was almost ethnic-looking, like a movie star in some Italian heavy breather. The sink was draining of water, steam hung around the bare bulb dangling from the ceiling.

"Where are you going?" I asked.

"I have a breakfast date, a tour of thrift shops and dive bars along Twenty-third Street." He dipped the shaving-cream brush into a coffee mug, soaping up the lather, swishing under his chin with the foamy bristles. I watched him like I used to watch my father. He smiled, a large gold cap covered his front tooth.

"Jennifer was looking for you," he said.

"Fuck Jennifer."

"Where'd you run off to?"

"I stopped by Mary's place."

"And?"

"And so maybe."

Robert opened the cabinet under the sink and pulled out a wooden cigar box. "If you're gonna go swimming in that pool, you better not be skinny-dippin'." He flipped the box open. It was full of condoms sealed in shiny foil packages. "Choose your shield," he said.

I picked out a gold coin.

"Heavy duty." He acted impressed. "You can always judge a man by his hood."

Part Two

New York

Courtney woke, felt cold air encircling her, pushed the sleeping bag aside, grabbed her coat, and tiptoed down the hallway, desperate to pee. The toilet was missing, so she went in the sink. There wasn't a mirror and, worse, there wasn't any toilet paper. Pulling up her pants, she spun the tap and let the cold water run a minute, rinsed her face in the same rusty sink, dried her hands on her pants, then walked back to Bobby's room, squatted in front of the space heater, warming herself in front of the red coils.

Bobby was snoring, his right arm hugging Courtney's pillow. An old Tuxedomoon song was playing upstairs, the distant violin haunting in the pale nacreous light. Courtney opened her bag, put on a clean T-shirt and her black wool sweater. She looked over at Bobby, kissed the palm of her hand, pressed it against his forehead, then grabbed her overcoat and hurried down the stairs.

Outside the temperature had crept up a few degrees, a silver helicopter droned overhead. She glanced into the bruise-colored sky, wiped her runny nose on the soft cuff of her sweater, tucked her chin into the fake-fur lining of her overcoat.

Two men dressed in black and white harlequin body-suits stood on the corner, their pointy hats had little bells that rang every time they moved, the taller one handed her a flyer as she passed.

"It's for a rave tonight in Williamsburg at an old candy factory," he said. "A labyrinth of sticky floors," camped the other.

Courtney glanced at the psychedelic rendering of a candy bar, then shoved it into her back pocket. She lit a cigarette and walked toward the Basement Cafe. Sitting in one corner of the dark room, she ordered coffee, then started tearing her paper napkin into little white squares. Flyers were taped to the wall advertising cheap airfares, sublets, and the need for drummers and bass players. A large ceiling fan stood idle, the walls were covered with sloppy art—stick men with gruesome faces in primary colors. Courtney checked her reflection in the window. She looked pale, softer in the tinted glass. Sunlight spread across the floor, a fat black cat soaked up its rays.

It was time for a drastic change, New York wasn't working for her. She was making the wrong connections in the wrong neighborhood with the wrong future. Staring out the window she watched all the sleepy people stutter up the block and thought about her old room in David's apartment. She wanted to blink and be back there, curled under blankets listening for his footsteps, the first scent of morning coffee, cigarettes, and toast.

"Hey Courtney!"

Courtney looked up.

"Jennifer? Shit, you scared the hell out of me. What are you doing here?" Courtney spun around, startled.

"I called last week and left a message with your boyfriend, told him I was coming this weekend. When I got into town last night I called you again, but he said you were at the Laundromat. You never returned my call, so I went by there this morning, rang the buzzer, finally this guy screams out the window, says you were kidnapped, tells me to go away or he'll blow up the building. What's that all about?"

"Tommy is fighting a dementia unknown to the common man." She pointed to her skull. "Anyway," she waved her hand as if she were turning a page, "that's over, long story, I'm so glad you're here!" Courtney reached up and hugged Jennifer.

"So where are you staying?"

"At a hotel on Forty-eighth Street." Jennifer sat down, unbuttoned her leather jacket.

"Sounds fancy." Courtney's eyebrows rose.

"It's not."

"This is so weird, I was just thinking about you. How

long are you here for?" Courtney asked, reaching for another cigarette.

"Just the weekend. I had to get out of Portland, everyone is driving me nuts." Jennifer glanced at the menu card,
swiveled in her chair to check out the room, ordered coffee.

"Tell me about it." Courtney laughed.

She'd known Jennifer since high school. They'd bonded
over a mutual smoking habit and a similar interest in skater
boys who hung out downtown after school. It seemed like
half their adolescence was spent sipping coffee, sifting the
bins at the used-record store, or rummaging through the
musty racks of thrift stores. When it came to boys, Jennifer
was better looking, so Courtney always had to be faster—
the first to get drunk, the first to have sex. These days she
thought of Jennifer as a diluted soft drink, flat with no fizz.
She hated that David was so goo-goo gaga over her.

"So what's new in the city of roses?" Courtney asked.
"Still hounding Robert?"

"Robert's an abstraction." She blinked. "He's there, but
he's not there."

"What do you mean?" She lit her cigarette.

"Well . . ." Jennifer hesitated, "we've never really slept
together."

"Oh," Courtney said flatly. She sipped her third coffee,
happy to have some company. If she played her cards right,
she could probably crash in Jennifer's hotel room and, if she
got lucky, Jennifer would turn out to be a good source of
cash.

The waitress set Jennifer's coffee on the table. "So what
about you? What's the deal with Tommy?"

"Well, like I said, I just broke up with Tommy. I'm staying with a friend of mine a few blocks from here until I can get my own place."

"Tommy who?" Jennifer asked, licking the sugar off her spoon, then stirring milk into her cup.

Courtney couldn't remember his last name. "Tommy," she said. "It's one of those singer things, you know, one name, like Cher or Sting or Madonna. It makes them seem immortal, God doesn't have a last name either."

Jennifer stared at the stick-figure art.

"I was sick of him anyway." She leaned toward Jennifer and whispered, "Can I borrow a couple of dollars? The cash machine ate my card this morning. I have tons of money in the bank, but I won't be able to get it out until Monday."

"Sure," Jennifer replied. "Is ten enough?" She looked into her purse.

"I'll pay you back right away, I promise." Jennifer handed her ten dollars. Courtney took the money, shoved it into her coat pocket.

"What do you want to do this afternoon?" Courtney asked.

"Let's go over to your new place. I'm dying to see a New York apartment." Jennifer blew on her coffee.

"Can't," Courtney said. "The landlord is painting today, that's why I'm here."

"Oh." Jennifer seemed disappointed, sipped at the edge of her cup.

A man across the aisle lit a match, held it between his thumb and forefinger, letting the flame extinguish itself in his skin. His face was dark and oily, his blazer covered with white cat hair. He stared at Courtney.

"She wasn't beautiful," he said, his hand shaking, "she was glamorous."

Courtney leaned toward Jennifer. "Psycho alert," she whispered. "We're outta here." Courtney stood up and put on her cat-eyed sunglasses. Jennifer paid the bill and met her outside. Courtney was wearing Jennifer's favorite purple hip-hugger flares.

"Aren't those mine?" Jennifer pointed.

"Are they?" Courtney blushed, turned away, and stretched.

A boy sped by on a bicycle and whistled at them.

"Fuck you!" Courtney yelled.

"Why'd you do that?" Jennifer asked. "He was kinda cute." Jennifer put on her sunglasses as well, smiled.

"Because it's demeaning to women. Feminism, heard about it?"

They walked toward Avenue A, staring into shop-windows.

"Say, why is that park all fenced up?" Jennifer asked, crossing the street. Blue barricades, like Tinkertoys, surrounded the square block of trees and grass.

"Because it's for the privileged, why do you think God made fences?"

Jennifer put her hands on the chain-link. "It's like they put nature in jail."

"They're gonna tear down the band shell."

"Why?"

"In any other neighborhood, it would be a historical

landmark, in this neighborhood, it's the only place some punk bands can get a gig."

"Why doesn't anybody do anything?"

"They're too busy shopping."

"Get away from there," a cop yelled, pointing at them.

"Excuse me!" Courtney yelled back.

"Do you believe in revolution?" Jennifer looked back at the cop.

"The only revolution I believe in is the wheels of a car headed straight out of town."

"Are you thinking of moving back to Portland?"

"It's so hard to live in New York, I can't even consider that it might be wrong." Courtney looked at Jennifer. "Seems like no matter where you live, you always want to be somewhere else."

The sky was a dirty blue streaked with the emissions of automobiles. Walking down Avenue B, people passed with their heads down. Two guys in black leather jackets were wheat-pasting flyers onto a lightpole, the one with the blue shag and oxblood lipstick made eyes at Jennifer.

"The boys in this neighborhood are seriously ugly," Jennifer said.

"The cruel facts of natural selection," Courtney pointed. "The East Village is brimming with white trash anxious to become folklore. Promise me you'll kill me if I'm still here in five years." Courtney shook Jennifer. "Promise me!"

"OK. I promise." They crossed the street.

"Everything you touch in this neighborhood is sticky," Courtney added.

"You hate it here, but you live here. You've always been

a woman of contradictions. You drink mineral water and smoke two packs of cigarettes a day."

"One pack," Courtney said, "and I'm gonna quit soon."

They followed Clinton Street to Delancey, weaving through slow-moving shoppers laden with plastic bags full of groceries.

"Have you had any luck starting a band?"

"A band? I can't even get a job. When I say I'm from Portland, everyone eyes me suspiciously, thinks I'm a criminal or something."

"I'm curious, because I've been thinking of moving here."

"Don't." Courtney kicked a stone.

"Why not?" Jennifer waved her arms.

"Too many bad influences."

"That's what David said."

Courtney thought of David, his long hair, his soul patch, the crazy all-night conversations. She remembered riding down the bus mall on his skateboard, freezing her butt off, squeezing him tight.

"I miss Portland so much," Courtney said. "It's so green. The last time I saw any nature was on television. I wish I could hike up to Washington Park right now," Courtney said in a dreamy voice, "and smell the rose garden, lay my head in the grass and sink my fingers into the warm soil."

"You make nature sound like phone sex," Jennifer said. "It's so boring! I don't want to spend the rest of my life watching sunsets. New York is dirty, everything is crooked, there's graffiti everywhere. It's such a relief."

All eight lanes of Delancey Street were clogged with

Saturday traffic. They walked up to the center of the steel
bridge. The sidewalk had deteriorated, there were giant
holes in the pavement. Green water lapped against the sea-
wall below. Courtney found an empty beer bottle and threw
it into the river. Sadness welled up inside her as she
watched its silent fall. She saw herself falling, twisting in the
wind. The bottle splashed silently against the din of traffic
noise and disappeared under the choppy water.

"When I die," she said, "I don't want a going-away
party." Her gums started to bleed, there was a ringing in her
ears. The sun slipped behind some clouds and the temperature began to drop. They walked off the bridge, which
shook and rattled as a subway train rumbled past, slinking
slowly into the Manhattan tunnel. Cars were racing toward
the traffic light, honking at the slightest hesitation. Vendors
were selling all kinds of junk on Delancey Street: plastic
dolls, cooked meat on a stick, and bootleg videotapes.
Courtney's feet were sore. Wiggling her toes, she felt the big
one poke through her sock.

"So what happened with Tommy?" Jennifer asked.

"Tommy lost his messenger job, started drinking. He
was always depressed, leaning over his manual typewriter
punching out lyrics for songs. His apartment was swarming
with cockroaches, hearing their little shells crack under his
shoe was one of the few pleasures he had. His father was in
the CIA, as a result, Tommy is a bit paranoid. He's got this
thing about espionage, thinks people are always following
him."

"Reminds me of David and his conspiracy theories,"
Jennifer said.

"How is David?" Courtney asked.

"Ugh, it's such a mess. After the fire he moved in with Robert and Tony."

"No way!"

"Yes way." Jennifer nodded. "We had a fight before I left town. I'll send him a postcard, he'll get over it."

"I wish someone would send me something." Her shoulders sagged.

"You're never in the same place more than a week, you're lucky I found you," Jennifer said.

"You're lucky you found me," Courtney replied. "I know of an excellent party tonight, should we go?" She pulled the candy bar flyer from her back pocket, showed it to Jennifer. They walked up Clinton Street, Spanish pop music blasting from a record store. Courtney stopped and bought a slice of pizza.

"You want one?" she asked.

Jennifer shook her head. "Too fattening."

Portland

I walked through the towering aisles of Powell's Books looking for an old Nelson Algren novel, the store isn't the same since the old man died. What happened to Powell's is what happened to Portland—the magic wand of gentrification sparkled over the city, big money moved up from L.A., all the seedy places were upgraded for the Yuppies in their Volvos. All the cool dive bars have been turned into discos or ice cream parlors, Powell's started selling *Vogue* magazine.

I found a hardcover copy of Richard Brautigan's *The Abortion* that had been discarded by the Multnomah County Library. Weird, because it's a story about a librarian who collects unwanted books by crazy people and now this copy has been abandoned by one. It had the worn look of a novel read several times, the spine was slanted, the orange jacket faded. Naturally, it was water-damaged, the blue stain seeping down the top of every page.

Powell's opened a cafe in the southwest corner of what used to be an auto dealer's showroom. I ordered a cup of coffee, sat at a table beside the window, stared at the cars swimming up Burnside. I used to romanticize Bohemian writers sipping cheap coffee in twenty-four-hour diners and think of bookstores as quasi-revolutionary hideouts where anarchists could soothe their beady eyes on the prison letters of Gramsci. Instead, they're crowded with college students typing into Powerbooks who think being radical means eating Ben & Jerry's ice cream. I wondered if all my romantic ideas would eventually fade and if so why I should ever fall in love. Watching traffic in and out of Three Queens, a boy bar across the street, I noticed a woman who looked like Mary pushing a baby carriage up the hill. Long black hair, straight bangs, skinny legs, the baby twisted the image and I realized I never thought of a girlfriend as the mother of my child.

The last sips of coffee had gotten cold so I tossed the paper cup in the can, slipped the Brautigan book under my jacket, and left the store, starting down Burnside toward Old Town. The overcast sky had broken and a whiskey sunlight reflected off the U.S. Bank Tower. I went into the lobby and used a pay phone to call the Green Tortoise, made a bus reservation. It's harvest season in southern Oregon, time to visit Phil.

Lisa walked into the lobby. I turned away so she wouldn't see me. Dressed in solid black, she looked like an assassin. Her hair was brushed back formal, and miniature chandelier earrings dangled beside her neck. She's probably on call for some fatso upstairs. A sudden uneasiness flooded over me. My crotch felt itchy. Lisa once gave me a bad case of crabs. They burrowed into my ballsack and I had to pick them out, one by one.

I made the reservation for the following day, then walked over to Fourteen NW Third. The go-go girls were just getting off work and the Heroin Bar was open downstairs. It was a tacky pisshole, smudged mirrors and cigarette burns on every surface. They played cheesy seventies disco music and charged a quarter to use the john. The red glow of Chinese altars hovered over the wicker-framed booths, woodsy-scented incense camouflaged the stench of burning narcotics. I bought a bag and rolled some in my tobacco. Mary walked over and kissed me. She had a handful of tips, was wearing a white halter top, a blue A-line miniskirt, white tights, and red high-top Converse All-Stars.

"You look very patriotic today," I said.

"Why thank you, want to go for a ride with my friends?" she asked, twirling a set of car keys.

"Sure."

We walked onto Third Street. Shopping-cart people were out in full force. One guy was selling wilted flowers, I bought a bouquet for a buck and gave it to Mary. She threw it on the dashboard. Two other girls got into the car, the three of them in front and me in back.

"I'm Spider." One of them turned around and faced me. "You got a smoke?" Spider was a gothic nightmare. She powdered her face white to look like a corpse and wore black lipstick, silver rings on every finger, a huge cross around her neck. She might as well have had fangs. I handed her a cigarette, she turned back around. The Burnside Bridge was up. We waited in line while a freighter full of logs floated toward Tokyo. I stared at the suicide hotline sign fastened to the bridge's guardrail. Someone had crossed out the phone number and scribbled JUMP! with black Magic Marker.

Spider turned on the radio, "92.3 KGON rocks!" The bridge went down, the flashing yellow light stopped, a speedmetal song crunched out of the speaker as we accelerated over the bridge, past the tattoo parlors and the old Irish bars near the mission. The line for supper already wrapped around the corner. I rolled down the window and let the cool mountain air blow over my face.

"Do you think Mt. Hood will blow up one day like Mt. St. Helens?" Spider asked.

"I hope so," Mary said. "I love disasters."

I thought about the night gray ash fell from the sky like snow, as if Heaven were on fire and this was the ashes of angels. In the morning the entire city was covered with powder. People roamed the streets wearing white masks, unsure whether the ash was toxic. The imprints in the ash made me think of footsteps on the moon.

Mary dropped off her girlfriends at another topless bar

in Northeast Portland. I got in the front seat and we drove back downtown.

"Where'd you get this car? It's a classic."

"I inherited it from my grandmother," Mary said, lighting two smokes, then handing me one.

"Your grandma must have been very cool."

"The coolest. She had an affair with John Reed."

"Really?"

"Yeah, but that other chick ran after him and got famous. We used to joke about how grandmother ended up with the dentist."

We sped past the industrial area along St. Helen's Road. The weeds beside the pavement were littered with garbage: bottles, paper cups, stuff thrown from cars. I fidgeted with the radio, leaned over and kissed her hand on the steering wheel, brushed my cheek against it, then laid my head in her lap.

"Sex with you is so intense," I said, emphasizing the last word.

"I went back on the pill," she said.

"Does that mean we're going steady?"

"Maybe." She shrugged, keeping her eyes on the road.

"I have some bad news," I said.

"What?" She looked down at me.

"I have to go to southern Oregon tomorrow."

"What for?"

"To see my film producer."

"How are you getting there?"

"Green Tortoise."

"Let's take my car!"

"Will it make it?"

"You wanna ride with a bunch of smelly hippies, go right ahead. I'll meet you down there. If those shitty old buses can make it, my grandma's car certainly can."

It started to drizzle. Mary put a tape in the cassette deck, an old Wipers song came on, "Romeo." She drove over the Sauvie's Island Bridge and turned left down a single-lane road surrounded by cow fields. Thin strands of barbed wire, post to post, split the fields.

Ahead, we came across four cars parked along the right-hand side of the road. Mary slowed down the car, pulled in behind them, and turned off the ignition.

"Are we going to a party?" I asked.

"No, baby, we're gonna pick some 'shrooms, c'mon." She opened her door, stepped out, walked around back, and opened the trunk. I looked over the field, saw two groups of people squatting in the grass. Mary slipped into a pair of baggy blue overalls, slammed the trunk, came around, and opened my door.

"C'mon, softy." She pulled my arm.

We crawled through the barbed-wire fence. The grass was wet and my wool socks were already squishing.

"Isn't this illegal?" I asked.

"Since when are you a keeper of the Ten Commandments?" She squatted, digging through the clumps of thick green grass, looking for clusters of little brown caps. The air was wet and my nose was running, I heard a shotgun in the distance.

"Hear that? They're shooting at us!" I said.

"Relax, they're pheasant hunters." Mary didn't look up,

she found a patch, and then another, plopping them into a
clear plastic Baggie. I wasn't having any luck. Spreading the
blades of grass, I found nothing.

"We split whatever we find, right?" I asked.

"No way," she said. "Finders keepers."

"Oh man!" I dug deeper and faster, trying to cover as
much square footage as possible, the knees of my jeans
now sopping wet, my hands muddy, my nose like a water
slide, totally jealous of Mary's bag of brown slime.

"Picking wild mushrooms really makes me feel like I'm
getting in touch with nature," Mary said.

"I'm getting in touch with misery."

"That's because you haven't found any mushrooms
yet," Mary said, not looking at me, plopping another batch
into her Baggie.

"You have to go slow, be patient, the mushrooms will
find you!"

I fingered through the fat blades of grass, trying to avoid
the cow pies. Up above, layer upon layer of leaky clouds
drizzled onto the moist fields dotted with cows, nervously
eyeing the strangers.

"Do you suppose the cows eat these mushrooms?"

"Sure," Mary said, keeping her eyes glued to the
ground.

"So all those cows over there are probably stoned out of
their minds?"

"Way."

I tried projecting myself into the mind of a stoned cow,
a sore jaw from chewing grass, swatting insects with a tail,
the heavy burden of sustaining the human race with vitamin

D, Ronald McDonald as Hitler's evil twin, the clumsy horror of a cow's existence. Whoa.

"Whatsamatter?" Mary asked.

"Nothing, maybe a little contact high. Can we go home now?"

"Give me a few more minutes, then I'll take you over to my parents' house."

"And meet your father?"

"My father won't be there, my parents are out of town."

I grabbed her hand, pushed her into the grass.

"Get off me!" She laughed.

I picked her up, carried her toward the fence.

"Let me down!" she yelled, kicking her legs.

More gunfire echoed through the woods. I dropped her in the muddy grass, stood, and lifted the barbed wire for her. "Please?" I begged.

Mary glanced back at the field, then stepped through the wire. She started the car and switched on the heat, pushed in the lighter. Shivering on the big bench seat, she lit two cigarettes, handed me one.

"We'll be there in a flash."

Mary pushed in The Wipers cassette. *Better Off Dead* rattled the tiny speakers. Greg Sage wails. I cranked it up, beating on the dashboard, jamming along with the drummer. Mary wiped the fog off the glass with a dirty white T-shirt. When she pulled away, I checked out her stash.

Her parents had a long gravel driveway. Nestled beside a row of tall pines and bushy evergreens was a

Tudor-style house, with a large picture window. Mary slid
the key into the slot, unlocked the door, turned on the
foyer light, and punched in the number code to deactivate
the silent alarm.

"Don't try and escape." She smiled, locking the door.
She threw her jacket on the red velvet sofa and headed
straight for the kitchen. I sat in a big black leather chair near
the fireplace, leafing through a book on the footrest called
The Trillion Dollar Debt.

"I'm going into the hot tub." She walked past me with
a bottle of red wine, two glasses, and her Baggie of
'shrooms. She opened the sliding glass door and stepped
out onto the deck, turned on the water jets, then lit three
purple candles and undressed. The water glowed blue like
television light, her toes skimmed the surface, testing the
hot bubbles. Mary's pale white skin was haunting in the
water's glimmering light, the liquid reflection rippling over
her body. She gritted her teeth and slipped in shoulder
deep, leaned over the side and poured the wine.

"Aren't you coming in?" she asked.

"I can't swim." I got up and walked over to her.

"You can stay in the shallow end," she said, "but swim
at your own risk, there's no lifeguard." As she sank deeper
into the pulsating water, her head went under, and her hair
spread over the surface like seaweed. She emerged, rested
her head on the edge of the tub, her blue eyes closed, her
breasts floating on the surface. I pulled off my shirt and
socks, unbuckled my belt. When I unzipped my jeans, her
eyes opened and she smiled. My hard-on flapped against
my stomach and I jumped right in. She picked up a glass of

wine and handed it to me, her other hand grabbed my penis under water.

"Why are we going to southern Oregon?" she asked, floating over me.

"Are you an FBI agent?" I asked.

"Of course," she said, squeezing my penis harder. "Talk, or else."

"I have a friend who grows weed. We have a scheduled meeting time at a gas station near his campsite. If I don't show up, he'll get totally paranoid."

"Ooh, a drug dealer." She laughed. "How sexy." Mary splashed up against me. "Hey Mister Naughty Drug Dealer, wanna fuck me in my daddy's bed?"

NewYork

"The *L* stands for losers." Courtney pointed at the sign above the black cement stairs descending into the subway. Steel bars painted yellow surrounded the dimly lit entrance. Jennifer bought a token from the woman behind the bullet-proof glass, Courtney jumped the turnstile.

"Pay your fare," the lady said through the crackling P.A. system, pushing a token under the glass to Jennifer.

Waiting on the platform, Jennifer sat on a bench, Courtney started drawing on a movie poster, putting little black hairs on Kim Basinger's legs.

"You don't know what pleasure this gives me," she said.

The train rolled in and they pressed into a crowded car. Courtney grabbed a silver pole and gazed at all the advertisements glowing above her: suicide, drug addiction, abortion, genital warts, AIDS, and torn earlobes. The train dipped into the tunnel for the stretch under the East River, the lights flickered on and off, she clutched Jennifer's arm in the strobe. Courtney saw a sweaty little man staring at her, turned her back to him.

"I feel like I'm riding down into Hell," Jennifer yelled over the noise.

Courtney turned toward her. "You are," she said.

They got out at the first stop, the aroma of urine hovered over the platform.

"Smell that?" Courtney asked. "That's the perfume of poverty." Courtney and Jennifer climbed the black stairs of the Bedford Avenue station and walked down Berry Street toward the party in the meatpacking district of Brooklyn. Steel hooks hung from the rafters in front of the brick warehouses, black pools of grease and watered-down blood stained the sidewalk, the stench of rotten meat lingered around the dumpsters.

"This neighborhood stinks," Jennifer said, holding her nose.

"Just imagine," Courtney said, "inside those refrigerated buildings are hundreds of slaughtered animals hanging from their feet, just like a horror movie."

Jennifer looked over at the buildings and shivered. "I don't eat anything with a face," she said.

"You don't eat anything, period," Courtney said.

They crossed the street and headed downhill toward the river.

"A lot of cute boys live over here," Courtney said, "painters and musicians, serious boys with ponytails and reading habits."

"Did I tell you a psycho killer moved in next door to me?" Jennifer asked.

"How do you know he's a psycho killer? Did you see his picture in *Psycho Killer* magazine or something?"

"I've seen him come home with huge green garbage bags."

"You watch way too much *Oprah*." Courtney laughed. "Maybe it's his laundry."

"That's what David said."

"Does David still hate me?" Courtney asked. Jennifer didn't answer. "The fire wasn't my fault," Courtney insisted. "I was in the bathtub at the time, surrounded by water."

"He thinks you did it on purpose, don't ask me why."

They turned another corner, a crowd was gathered in front of a four-story red-brick warehouse. A large plastic banner hung over the entrance, the same psychedelic candy bar insignia as on the flyer. People were drinking beers, leaning on parked cars. Courtney took Jennifer's hand and led her toward the door, pushing past others, waving her invites at the tall skinny boy standing near the entrance holding a clipboard and sweating nervously.

"I have passes," she yelled.

"We all have passes." Some fat biker chick pushed her back.

The doorman waved at Jennifer, bouncers pushed people aside to let her and Courtney into the building. Courtney grabbed Jennifer's hand, stepped past the biker bitch, winked at her boyfriend.

"That was easy," Jennifer said.

"Beauty goes a long way in this town."

The room was very dark. Old candy trucks were parked along the back wall, clown paintings flaked from their side panels. Strobe lights stuttered over the crowded dance floor, techno music blasting. Courtney and Jennifer leaned against a wall trying to get their bearings, letting their eyes adjust to the darkness. A boy with dreadlocks walked past them, they both turned their heads.

"Do you think I'll ever fall in love?" Jennifer yelled over the music.

"I thought you were in love?" Courtney replied cynically.

"No, I mean really in love, like I'm gonna die or something."

"Like Romeo and Juliet?" Courtney asked. Jennifer nodded.

"What good is love if you have to die for it? Love comes, it's never found. You can't go out and get love, you have to lure it in, like a fisherman."

"I've been fishing for years," Jennifer said, "but I always throw them back."

"Why?" Courtney asked. "Too small?"

"All the fish I catch are inedible."

"Maybe you're fishing in the wrong pond?" Courtney smiled.

"Or using the wrong bait," Jennifer said sadly. "Do you like my haircut?"

"Love it," Courtney said.

Jennifer was wearing her green suede jacket, a sheer black dress with little white stars, black tights, and her silver Saturn necklace which she clutched nervously whenever somebody interesting passed.

"Do you really think Robert is gay?" she asked.

Courtney was staring at a Rasta boy across the room. She rolled her eyes. "Robert is a dog, he'll sniff anything."

Jennifer made a face like a sliver had pierced into her heart.

"This place is full of models," Courtney said in disgust. "You want a drink?"

Jennifer nodded and followed her to an old assembly line that was serving as a bar top. The bartender had long tangled red hair and freckled skin, a small silver cross hung over a tight black T-shirt, a Thrasher tattoo colored his upper arm.

"Two vodka tonics," Courtney ordered.

When he turned his back, Courtney leaned over the bar to check out his buns. Jennifer scanned the crowd.

"What do you think?" Courtney asked Jennifer, nodding toward the bartender.

"I don't like guys with bigger tits than me," she said.

"You got any X?" Courtney asked the bartender as he set the drinks in front of her.

"How many?" he asked. She flashed him a peace sign.

"One plus one is twenty," he said, laying two small white envelopes on the bar. Courtney scooped them up, turned to Jennifer.

"Pay the man," she said.

Jennifer shifted through her purse, handed a twenty to the bartender.

"The drinks are on the house." He smiled.

"I'll be back for you later." Courtney winked.

Jennifer followed Courtney into the bathroom. Four women crowded around three separate mirrors, brushing their hair, glossing their lips.

"What's that thing JFK told Marilyn?" Courtney asked. "Never before have so many people wasted so much time to accomplish so little." She pointed at the women in front of the mirror. Jennifer went into a stall and locked the door. Courtney knocked.

"Let me in, stupid."

Jennifer opened the door. "I gotta go!"

"So go!" Courtney ordered, locking the door behind her. Jennifer lifted her skirt and pulled down her black tights. Courtney opened one of the small white envelopes.

"So many people come to New York to get rich," Courtney said. "They should come to New York to kill the rich!"

"Shut up, you're giving me shy bladder."

"In Africa people are starving for food, in New York they're starving for attention." Courtney licked her finger and dipped it in the powder, rubbed some on her gums. Jennifer stood, wiped, and pulled up her tights. Courtney handed her an envelope.

Jennifer rubbed some of the white powder onto her tongue, took a sip of her drink, kept an ice cube in her mouth, crushed it with her teeth. She rolled up a dollar bill and snorted the rest.

"Whoa," she said, sniffling, wiping her nose.

"Ready?" Courtney asked. Jennifer nodded.

They walked out of the bathroom, Jennifer checking herself in the mirror behind Courtney. The dance floor was crowded and dark, large projections of cartoon characters were on the walls. It was very hot inside and Courtney started to sweat.

"Why is Robert so indifferent to me?" Jennifer yelled.

"Forget about Robert," Courtney yelled back.

"How can I get his attention?" she asked. "It's like he has no feelings."

"You talking about a zombie or your boyfriend?" Courtney asked.

"He irritates the hell out of me."

A young woman walked past. "Check out those shoes." Courtney pointed at red, white, and blue platforms.

"You're such a seventies whore," Jennifer said. "Looks like something Peter Frampton would wear." They leaned against a candy truck. "He looks yummy." Jennifer pointed out a guy who was smiling at them. "You want another drink?" she asked. Courtney nodded. "I'll be right back."

When Jennifer walked away, Mr. Smiley approached Courtney. He wore an extra large skater T-shirt untucked over baggy blue overalls, and Airwalk sneakers, his long knotted hair bleached blond at the tips and pushed to one side. Several cloth Indian bracelets covered one wrist, a string of multicolored wood beads were tied around his neck.

"Where'd your friend run off to?" he asked, looking at Jennifer.

"Friend? She's some raging lesbian who's been hitting

on me all night, thank God you arrived." She grabbed his arm. "Wanna dance?" Courtney pulled him onto the dance floor, squeezing between the shaking bodies.

"How do you like my party?" he shouted, waving his arms over the crowd.

"This is your party? You sure have a lot of friends." She smiled, the X was coming on, her vision started to crystallize. The colored lighting and the plastic plants in the middle of the dance floor made her feel like she was floating in a crowded fish tank.

"What's your name?" she asked, glancing around for Jennifer.

"Louis."

"I'm Courtney."

"Are you a Scorpio?" he asked.

"How did you know?"

"Sylvia Plath was a Scorpio."

"So?"

"You look a lot like Sylvia Plath."

She looked at the crows-feet slithering away from the edges of his eyes and guessed he was in his late twenties, that he had some money, that he probably went to college. When the song mixed into a faster ambient groove, he leaned close, his breath on her ear.

"The sign of water," he whispered, "of night, of intelligence, of anguish and suicide."

Courtney felt herself getting lighter, she danced harder, kept her eyes off him.

"Let's go up on the roof," he said, taking her hand. "It's too hot down here."

Courtney looked once more for Jennifer, then followed him up the silver staircase through a doorway that opened onto the roof. Several other couples were already up there, holding hands, making out. The roof overlooked the entire city. There was no end to it, heat lightning flashed beyond the transmission wires, a subway train crossed the Williamsburg Bridge. In the opposite direction an amusement park twinkled through the street-lit marmalade-colored sky. Up above: one or two stars, planes in line to land at La Guardia, the air heavy with diesel smoke. Courtney rubbed her eyes.

"You can see the Earth's skin from up here," Louis said.

"Looks like a lot of acne," she said, the roof thumping from the music downstairs. "As pretty as it is, it kind of makes me sad."

"Why?"

"Look over there." She pointed. "All the windows are sealed with iron bars. It's as if God really was dead and some people already know it."

Louis leaned over the ledge, looked down onto the street. "Law and order can't save nobody anymore," he said, "they're just around to pick up the pieces."

"So where are you from?" she asked.

"Brazil."

"Brazil like the rain forest or Brazil like the movie?"

"Somewhere in between."

"So why would someone like you want to move to Williamsburg?"

"To meet you," he said.

"Yeah right." Courtney blushed, noticed a woman near the stairwell staring at her.

When Courtney caught her eye, she turned and disappeared into the dark throbbing walls. Old girlfriend, she thought, looking down at the street, watching a group of girls getting out of a white limousine. She was spacing out, shook her head, a cool gust of wind made her shiver. "I'm cold, let's go back downstairs." She pulled his silver jacket. "I want to dance." She clutched Louis's hand and led him back downstairs. The crowd was a mass of elbows and knees, strange bodies pressed against her, one deep heartbeat of aggressive trancelike music.

Louis pushed a capsule between Courtney's lips, then pulled a small bottle of Rémy from his jacket. He took a long swig, passed the bottle to her. Blue perfumed smoke filled the room. Courtney took off her jacket, let it fall in front of her, took a fast swig, and passed the bottle back. The hot whiskey rushed down her throat and burned inside her chest. She glanced left and right. Louis pulled Courtney close to him, face to face, then kissed her once, twice, again. Soft volleys of moist lips pressed against her and suddenly she felt very horny. He reminded her of David in a weird way—slightly underfed, pale, bangs that kept falling into his eyes.

"Stop it," she said playfully, pushing him away. She blushed and looked again for Jennifer. Louis swayed drunkenly, tugging at her belt loops, staring at her breasts. He leaned into her, grabbed her ass, and pressed his crotch against hers. Courtney could feel his erection and let her head fall back as he kissed her neck. She pushed him away, shivered, closed her eyes, started dancing again. Louis's advances took the pace of waves. He pressed up against her and kissed her again, "like a flower," she thought. Courtney swayed, sweaty from dancing, the crowd became a blur of faces.

"I'm tired, can we go sit somewhere?" she asked.

"You want to go up to my office?" he asked. Courtney shrugged, picked up her jacket, and followed him toward the back. It was a large unlit building full of empty candy trucks. They turned left, then right, suddenly there was no light at all. The music got farther away, Louis opened the door of a truck.

"You first," he said.

"This is your office?" she asked.

Courtney climbed onto the front bench seat. Louis climbed in beside her. He took a little white envelope out of his shirt pocket and spilled its contents onto the dashboard.

"No more X for me," she said. "I'm wasted."

"It's coke," he said. "It'll pick you up a bit." Louis rolled up a fifty-dollar bill, handed it to Courtney. He split the pile into four thin lines using his credit card. Courtney bent over and snorted one.

"Wow," she said, suddenly very high. "You sure that was coke?" She felt a strange burning sensation in the back of her throat. The truck got blurry and Courtney reached for the door handle, feeling like she was going to throw up. She leaned over the glove compartment, started rolling down the window, swayed, tried to focus, then puked over the dashboard.

"Fuckin' A," Louis yelled. Courtney tried to wipe off her pants, got the spins, thought she was gonna pass out. He swore at her in Spanish. She felt scared, far away from anyone she really trusted.

"I'm sorry," she said. "I'm really sorry."

Louis opened the glove compartment, found some paper napkins, and handed them to her. Courtney wiped off her face, saw a black handgun in there, a plastic Baggie of white powder, and a rubber-banded roll of money. Courtney was scared, her body felt heavy, like a stove was pressing down upon her. Louis climbed into the back of the truck, then reached over the seat and put his hands under Courtney's armpits, pulled her over the seat and into the back of the truck. It was absolutely black. She felt his smooth hands sliding over her legs, her sweaty stomach, and then her bra. She couldn't make a fist, couldn't even feel her hand. He unzipped her pants and pulled them down, laid on top of her, rubbed his cock against her. She shivered, trying to clear the blur swallowing her eyes.

"No," she said, her tongue dry and swollen. He put his hand over her mouth. Courtney was afraid of suffocating, afraid that he would hurt her, the sweet smell of cotton candy filled her head.

"Please don't kill me," she thought.

She reached out, her long fingers extended, there was nothing to grab onto. He rolled her over, pulled her arms back, then spread her legs. Her body shook as he entered her pussy from behind, her face rubbing against the rubber mat on the floor. He leaned over her, pressed down upon her, his smelly breath blew past her face and she thought she would puke again. She dry-heaved, closed her eyes, and blacked out.

*   *   *

When she woke, her pants were curled around her ankles, her shoes still on, her T-shirt moist from sweat and vomit. She felt patches of sticky sperm on her upper thigh and started to cry. The truck was pitch black, she couldn't see in the dark, a white fuzziness glowed at the edge of her eye. Louis was gone. Still numb, her head was swirling. She stood up, stumbled forward, and fell, banging her elbow on the floor. Reaching up, she felt the bench seat and lifted herself up, pulled her pants back over her waist, crawled over the bench seat, and opened the door. White light spilled over the dashboard, she squinted her eyes. The glove compartment was empty. Courtney found some napkins on the floor, wiped off her hands and face, then stepped cautiously onto the cement floor. Dizzy, she followed the sound of music back toward the main room, edging alongside the crowd, trying not to face anyone, working her way toward the bathroom. In the mirror she saw vomit pasted on one cheek, leaned over the sink, turned on the faucet, splashed her face, scooped the water into her mouth, then went into a stall and sat on the toilet. She peed, got up to flush, the water was pink.

"Oh fuck," she mumbled, the events speeding backward with the immediacy of a car crash. She opened the door, felt weightless as tissue paper, lost her balance, and collapsed onto the floor, her face pressed against the cool white tile.

Portland

When I got home Robert was on the futon watching one of Sheila's videos, his feet in fuzzy slippers, a martini in his left hand.

"If it isn't the six-o'clock sadist." I closed the door, pulled off my shoes.

"Sit down and watch a little porno with Robby, you might learn something."

"It's so boring." I looked over and saw a biker bar scene, two guys in chaps shooting pool, obviously the action hadn't started yet, the film still muddled in character development.

"Yes, but all the panting relieves my headache," he said. "C'mere, sit next to me." He patted the futon.

I went into the kitchen to make some coffee. Found the french roast in the freezer, checked my acid stash buried beneath the ice-cube trays. The refrigerator was covered with local band stickers, Polaroids—a "been-there, done-that" tombstone.

"The vice squad came by today," Robert said nonchalantly. "I wasn't here, but Tony said they were investigating an illegal nightclub at this address that apparently catered to minors. Tony told them we were good Christians and that they must be referring to one of our fellowship drives." Robert cracked up. "They searched the building."

"Did they have a warrant?" I asked.

"Doubt it." Robert tapped his long leg, his arms folded around his sequined T-shirt, nervously fingering a Virginia Slims.

"So how did the cops find out?" I asked.

"Christ, it couldn't have been that hard, all they had to do was drive by on any given night. Maybe somebody sent them an invitation."

I lit a cigarette. The water boiled and coffee trickled into the glass pot.

"Since when is it illegal to have a party?" I asked.

"Since whenever the cops get a stick up their butt," Robert said, staring at the screen, the television now oohing and ahing. "Which reminds me, Sheila's opening is tonight, should we go?"

"Sure, let me take a shower first."

"I'll get the camera." Robert smiled.

We walked down to Occupied Space, a gallery in the warehouse district. The building was hurriedly constructed at the height of World War II by a shipbuilder who anticipated making a fortune when Japanese submarines were discovered lurking off the coast of Oregon. The guy went bankrupt when the atomic bomb was dropped on Hiroshima and the war suddenly ended. The city took it over and turned it into a nonprofit gallery space for local artists. Unfortunately, there's a cat food factory across the road and when the wind blows from the north, the heavy fetid smell of roasted Mr. Ed fills the air.

"What's Sheila's new show called?" I asked.

"Twenty-first-Century Decadence."

"Did you help her with any of the research?"

"Apparently they're just photographs of large spectacles: fashion shows, rock concerts, football games, and parades. She told me on the phone that this was her last show because she can't take art seriously anymore, its inevitable meaninglessness is so overwhelming."

"What do you call her art?"

"Post-Depressionism."

Robert walked very slowly, his clogs clucking every delicate step, his hands wrapped securely around his chest. He was very handsome and not shy about reminding anyone. His striking beauty had opened a lot of doors for him, but at the same time left him detached, hypercynical, irreverent, and easily bored. He disses everyone, treating lovers like laundry, a new outfit every season. Robert publishes a fanzine called *Stupid,* so everyone in town owes him a favor. He's a bit of a slut, but nearly everyone in Portland is, it's a very incestuous town.

Robert treated me like a little brother, guiding me down the sidewalk hoping I'd find my way. Tony, on the other hand, kept a distance. Older and less handsome, he was too wound up in his own emotional crisis, trying to keep Robert's attention. The weird thing is, they were the only real couple I knew. I went out of my way to pay back their hospitality, always doing the dishes, keeping beers in the fridge. They were constantly bickering, but when it came to me, they were both perfect gentlemen, as if it were some kind of bitch contest to win my favor.

We stopped for an imported beer at a deli and sipped them as we strolled down Twelfth Street. Robert used a straw.

"So why do you lead Jennifer on?"

"I don't lead her on, she leads herself on." Robert wrapped the brown paper bag tighter around his bottle. "She clings to me because she's got a Cinderella complex and wants to keep her options open. I'm just the social director. She knows I'm not interested."

"No she doesn't."

Robert checked his reflection in a used bookstore window. "She's a good source of capsules, otherwise the girl's just ornamentation, what do you see in her anyway? She's too obsessed with herself to ever be committed to anyone. Courtney is the real thing." He took a sip of his beer. "Why do you think Jennifer is so attracted to her?"

I took a pull off my beer, saw my own reflection in the glass. My face looked bloated, older, droopy even.

"But maybe your female trouble is a cover for your own sexual ambiguity? We're not having a crisis, are we?" He took a sip of his beer, smiled.

"Robert, if I turn colors, you'll be the first to know. Promise."

"Well, if it's any consolation, I don't do girls." He shuddered, then opened the gallery door.

We walked into the brightly lit room, already packed with chain-smoking art rats. Lisa broke out of the crowd, made a beeline toward us.

"Hey Robert," she said, smiling, ignoring me. "What's new?"

"Same old dust balls, I'm afraid." He glanced around the room.

"Maybe I could come over and do some vacuuming." She made a weird sucking noise. The girl had no inhibitions. Robert looked annoyed.

"My fireman friends have been telling stories," he said.

"What fireman friends?" she asked.

"They say you called in a five-alarm fire and when they broke down your door you were on the bed, masturbating no less."

"That's a lie!" she screamed, her face turning beet red.

"They say it wasn't the first time. I know there's some heat between those legs but, girlfriend, firemen? Really!"

"The only extinguisher I'm interested in is yours." She reached for Robert's crotch.

"Ouch!" He backed away, made eyes at a tall blond boy staring at the monster trucks exhibit.

"Excuse me," I said. "I'm going to look for a john."

"Give David the number of yours." Robert tapped Lisa's shoulder. She hit him on the arm with her handbag.

The bathroom was jammed, a long line was forming around the fast-food collages and supermodel trading cards. I went outside to piss in the street. Several years worth of band posters were stapled to the telephone poles. They looked like swollen bellies. I unzipped my fly and peed on one, the hot yellow water steamed against the oil-soaked wood, pooling in hunks of green moss growing on the sidewalk. I aimed higher and accidentally doused a Poison Idea poster, right on Jerry A.'s face. Oops, sorry man. I leaned closer and fire-hosed Pearl Jam. Aah! I had a sudden urge to go all over town dusting bogus rock stars, calmed myself over a cigarette, then wandered slowly back inside.

A flashbulb popped in one corner, Robert stood beside Sheila as local press worked the crowd. People seemed more interested in the free drinks than art. Conversations were interrupted by flirtatious glances, everyone seemed to be on the make. Sheila was talking about her friend's abortion, how she videotaped it, that copies were for sale at the door.

"I'm gonna send it to the NEA as a grant proposal," she said. Everyone laughed.

"This is a wonderful collection." Robert stared at the

walls. "I particularly like that one." He pointed at a photograph of a sweaty shirtless rock star, his tongue extended and his guitar resting on his hip as if he were jerking it off.

"You would," Sheila said.

"Rock stars are a showcase of American ingenuity," Robert said.

"So are serial killers." Sheila took both of our arms. "C'mere, I want you guys to see my new film. We stepped through a red satin curtain into a small backroom and sat on some folding chairs in the last row. "We don't have to watch the whole thing," she said. "You'll get the idea pretty quickly."

Some nature girl was getting it in the ass from a lumberjack.

"The sound effects are awesome," Robert said.

"It's called *Treehuggers,*" she said. "The women go out and hug trees to stop lumberjacks from cutting them down, when that doesn't work, the women fuck the lumberjacks so many times they're too tired to cut any trees."

"Whoa," I said. "Very p.c."

"Hey you, shut up," some guy yelled from the front.

Sheila shrugged, led us back into the gallery. I checked the movie poster for familiar faces.

"So what's your new film about?" Sheila asked.

"Two superheroes called the Minister of Disco and the Ambassador of Love."

"What's it called?" she asked.

"The Unbearable Lightness of Portland," Robert cut in. We laughed.

Sheila floated off to prospective collectors, Robert made

another pass at the tall blond, I went into the hallway and called Mary, left a message on her machine. It's nice to know you're lingering in someone's living room, waiting for them to come home. The room was getting crowded, so I went outside. Robert came out behind me, bummed a smoke, lit my cigarette with his antique lighter, some gas station giveaway from the fifties. I could never understand his infatuation with that era, he seemed so modern. Sometimes I wondered if it wasn't role-playing, pretending to be his own father. When I asked he acted nostalgic. "Quality," he said. "It was a much better world."

Lisa rolled up on her motorcycle, wearing a little red cowboy jacket with black fringe running up the sleeve.

"This town is slowing down around me." She stared at Robert. "I'm hitting the dusty trail in search of some real men."

"There goes your taxi." Robert pointed at a garbage truck driving down Glisan Street. I cracked up. Lisa put her bike in gear and rode away.

"That girl's a real piece o' work," Robert said. "She'd lift her skirt for a compliment."

"I'm going home," I said.

"Come to the Wild West for a while," Robert asked coyly. "A mind is an important thing to waste. I'll buy you a drink."

I hesitated, then followed along hoping to run into Mary.

We walked down Glisan to the Wild West. Drag queens were dancing on the bar, fluorescent-green stockings under black light, shiny vinyl bras, and long curly wigs, the makeup spread thick to last. The front bar was packed, Robert pulled me into the dj booth. Nightclubs are like drugs, the experience is completely based on mood. Robert handed me a vodka tonic. It too glowed fluorescent green under the black light, like I was sipping toxic waste.

Sugar and Spice were performing on the stage, two bald queens in skintight black rubber outfits. A Super-8 film was projected on the rear wall behind them, showing one man sucking another's toes, rose petals fell from the ceiling. Spice sprayed rosy air freshner into the crowd, then wrapped a rubber hose tightly around Sugar's arm and injected a syringe to extract blood. Slowly, the glass vial filled with red blood. Records were spinning backwards, a strange haunting sound warbled from the small P.A. Spice pulled the needle from Sugar's arm and squirted the blood into his mouth, then over his forehead. Blood trickled over his face. They embraced each other and kissed furiously. Sugar lit a fuse with a butane lighter. The flame curled down to a small pile of gunpowder, which sparked, then gushed into a puff of pink smoke billowing over the stage. The lights went out and the audience applauded. Music came back on, Silver Convention's "Fly Robin Fly." I looked over at Robert, he was leaning out of the dj booth talking to a stranger.

 New York

"Speed bump," a woman warned her friend as they walked into the bathroom, stepping over Courtney. "That girl needs makeup therapy," said the other, both of them laughing as they wiggled into a single booth.

Courtney pushed herself up off the floor, leaned against the wall, pressed her hands against her knees, taking deep breaths. She leaned over the sink, ran cold water and spooned handfuls into her mouth. In the mirror she saw Jennifer coming into the bathroom. Quickly, she buried her face in a brown paper towel.

"Courtney, where have you been? I've been looking all over for you. So many gorgeous men are hitting on me out there." Jennifer checked herself in the mirror, then glanced at Courtney.

"You don't look so good, are you sick?"

Courtney nodded, felt her chin trembling. "The full moon is making me edgy, c'mon, we're outta here." Courtney turned and pushed open the bathroom door, needled her way through the crowd, Jennifer right behind her.

Outside, the air was chilly, a line of yellow cabs idled along the curb. A large crowd still pressed toward the door, arms raised, anxious to make eye contact with the doorman.

"Where's Louis?" Courtney asked him.

"Who are you?" he replied.

"I'm his girlfriend."

He laughed, looked back at the crowd. "Louis got a lot of girlfriends," he said.

Courtney pushed her way through the crowd, Jennifer tagging close behind. Two boys wearing baseball caps were making out across the street. On the corner, several more were peeing silently against a garage door.

"Why were you crying in the bathroom?"

"What are you talking about?" Courtney turned away from Jennifer.

"You were crying."

"No I wasn't."

"Courtney." Jennifer grabbed Courtney's arm. "Did that guy mess with you?"

"I don't want to talk about it." Courtney pulled away.

"Did he?" Jennifer yelled.

"Drop it, Jennifer."

"No."

"I threw up, OK?" Courtney stared at her, then turned and started walking. "It was too crowded, I couldn't breathe." She stopped at a bodega. "I'm gonna get some water, you want anything?"

Jennifer shook her head.

"Then wait here." Courtney went in and bought a disposable douche, a pack of Dentyne, and a bottle of seltzer water. She put the douche in her overcoat pocket before going outside where Jennifer was waiting, silent and annoyed.

"C'mon, we'll take the subway," Courtney said, stepping down the greasy stairs into the dimly lit corridor. She looked both ways, then jumped the turnstile.

"Pay your fare," said the old Black man from inside the booth, the loudspeaker echoed in the empty station. Jennifer bought a token and put it in the slot. The smell of ammonia rose from the pavement, the bench was occupied by a sleeping man using a loaf of bread as a pillow. Courtney leaned against the steel pillar, sipping her water.

Everything had happened so fast, she could still smell his whiskey breath, still feel his rough hands. He raped her, but she might have fucked him anyway. Her shoulders were tense, her neck sore, she wrapped her overcoat tighter around her waist.

"Are you OK?" Jennifer asked. "You seem kinda upset."

"I didn't like the party, OK?" She turned away, stared into the black hole where the tracks disappeared.

A wind came up through the tunnel and two headlights appeared, Courtney stepped behind the yellow line. The train squealed to a stop, the doors opened, and they both got on. Two teenage boys sitting opposite one another checked out Courtney and Jennifer as they entered the otherwise empty car. The doors closed and the train lugged forward, dipping under the East River.

Courtney ran both her hands through her hair. She felt light-headed, the scent of cheap aftershave and boozy boy-sweat made her sick to her stomach. She leaned back, banged her head against the glass, stared at Jennifer. *Why didn't it happen to her? Why is her life so easy?* She wanted to scream, pushed her folded hands between her legs, squeezed them together. She wanted to take a shower, to brush her teeth. She wanted to go home, realized she didn't have one, sunk deeper into herself. She pressed her hands against her face, smelled the sweat of her palms, took long deep breaths.

The train burst into the First Avenue Station. The doors shuddered open. Courtney and Jennifer stepped onto the platform.

Outside the sky was overcast, the city light reflected in the clouds a pale dishwater gray. A gas crew drilled the street, steam rose from the crevice. Cars honked jockeying for position at the red light. Jennifer took a deep breath and let out a heavy sigh.

"I gotta pee like a racehorse." Courtney crossed her legs, noticed a church across the street. The stained glass windows looked warm and inviting. "Let's go in there for a minute and warm up." Courtney pointed at the church. She took Jennifer's hand and they ran across the street. A dim orange light lit the entrance, two saints stared from columns on opposite sides, a pattern of cement angels arched over the doorway. Courtney pulled the heavy door open and walked hesitantly through the narthex, then up the center aisle to a wood pew. Kneeling on a prayer bench, she blessed her mother who lost her sanity, prayed it wasn't hereditary.

Wind rattled the stained glass windows, dark orange streetlight glowed behind them. Jennifer went over to a side altar, lit one of the white prayer candles.

Courtney closed her eyes and listened to a soft shimmer of steam rise into the radiators from the boiler downstairs. She thought of her first Communion, the shiny black Mary Jane shoes she wore to bed the night before, afraid they would run away, how when the priest tipped the chalice to her lips, she got excited, tipped the base too far, and stained her little white dress.

She smelled rotting vegetables, rubbed her nose, opened her eyes. An old man in a gray overcoat knelt beside her. Certain she was about to be flashed, Courtney inched away, patted her pockets for a cigarette, started gnashing her teeth. She tried to be nice, Jesus, after all, was a homeless man.

"People sleep late when they're depressed," he said, "because, in essence, they want to die." Courtney looked at the ceiling. A large fresco was painted above the altar, Jesus rising on a golden cloud surrounded by angels.

"The mind reacts"—he pointed to his head—"creates dreams to propagate hope." He raised his eyebrows and leaned closer to Courtney.

"Do you have a dream you'd like me to interpret?" he asked.

"I don't sleep," she said, getting up, "but thanks anyway."

Courtney wandered back into the narthex, found a bathroom, and went into a stall. She ripped open the paper box containing the douche. The girl on the box looked very seventies. Standing in a field holding flowers, she reminded her of Susan Dey. Courtney tore open the plastic bag encasing the nozzle, twisted off the tab on the douche, and screwed down the nozzle. She straddled the toilet, eased the nozzle into her pussy, and squeezed the plastic container, felt the cold vinegar-water jet against the walls of her vagina, streams of water gushed over her hand and poured into the toilet. Courtney patted herself dry with toilet paper, pulled her pants up, wrapped her panties in a paper towel, and threw them in the garbage. She went down the center aisle, saw the old man crashed out in a pew and Jennifer staring at the floating saints painted on the wall.

"See anybody you know?" Courtney asked.

"Religion is so psychedelic," Jennifer said. "The stories are so bizarre, like the one about the ark, all the animals, all the rain."

"Reminds me of Portland," Courtney said. "C'mon, let's get outta here, churches give me the willies." She glanced over her shoulder. "Why does God want his house so spooky anyway?" Jennifer followed and they were back on First Avenue.

"Do you believe in reincarnation?" Jennifer asked.

"I did until history class in high school, none of the pictures in my textbook looked familiar and I realized it was all a hoax. I mean, if I were here before this time, I'd have some response to those pictures, am I right?"

"But what if you were a bug or something?"

"I didn't get a buzz in science class either."

They walked past a pizza parlor, Courtney stopped and stared at the boy twirling dough like a giant Frisbee, matting it with his hands. She looked at Jennifer, then pointed at two boys in silver pants groping one another in front of the bar next door. "Look, there's Robert," she said.

"Where?"

"Just kidding, you want a slice?"

"No thank you."

"What do you eat, air?"

Jennifer ignored her, staring at the two boys. Courtney came out with a slice on a white paper plate. She smiled, took another bite. "I live on this stuff," she said.

"I noticed."

"It's getting kinda late." Courtney glanced at her watch-less wrist.

"Yeah, I'm beat," Jennifer said. "You wanna come up to my hotel room?"

"Can I crash there?" Courtney asked.

"Of course." Jennifer held her hand up trying to flag down a cab.

"I was thinking," Courtney said with her mouth full of food, "that maybe I'd go back with you for a visit."

"Really?" A cab stopped in front of them, Courtney opened the door.

"Yeah, why not. I have an open ticket, and I'm afraid if I don't use it, I'll lose it. Would it be OK to stay with you? I don't really have anywhere else to stay."

"Uh," Jennifer hesitated as she climbed into the black interior, scooting over to make room for Courtney, "sure, I guess."

"Where to, ladies?" the cabbie asked. A car honked behind him. The driver flashed his brights on and off.

"Forty-eighth and Broadway," Jennifer said. The cab jerked forward, accelerating through a series of green lights. Courtney leaned back into the seat, relieved, watching the street numbers climb.

"I haven't shown you yet." Jennifer lifted the side of her skirt, pulled down the elastic band of her tights and showed Courtney the purple daisy tattoo on her hip.

"Where'd you get that?"

"In Northeast Portland, Robert took me."

"Cool."

"If I'm ever dead, that's how you'll know it's me, OK?" She pulled her tights back up, straightened her dress.

"Sure." Courtney looked over at Jennifer, tried not to laugh.

The cab stopped in front of the Marriott. Courtney followed Jennifer through the lobby and onto a glass elevator. "This place must have been designed by the same guy who did the *Love Boat,* check out all the ferns," Courtney said as the glass tube ascended.

Jennifer's room was at the end of the hall, the musty air-conditioning was cranked. She turned on the lights and opened the mini-bar, cracked a Heineken. "You want one?" Jennifer asked.

"Nah." Courtney went to the window, pulled back the curtains to check out the view.

The room's decor was American sci-fi, lots of mirrors and chrome trim. The artwork was screwed down to the wall, as if anyone would want to steal it.

"This room has more furniture than my apartment." Jennifer propped up some pillows, lay down on the bed, reached for the remote on the nightstand, and turned on the idiot box. Balancing the Heineken on her stomach, she started surfing channels. Courtney stared out the window overlooking Eighth Avenue, the storefronts a string of sex shops, videos, live one-on-ones. Cars lined up one after the other, their headlights beaming, like a continuous funeral procession circling the block. Recalling the night's events, she squeezed her legs together, wishing it all away, then crossed the room, propped two pillows beside Jennifer, and curled onto the bed, lying on her side, hands tucked under the pillow.

Jennifer took a hit of her beer, kept surfing, settled on a soft porn flick: a calendar boy and matching bimbette pressing their bodies together in the greatest fuck of all time.

"It's never that good," Jennifer said and went on surfing,

pausing on the wedding scene from *The Graduate*. "Do you think a woman's greatest fear is that she'll never get married?"

"No. I think it's whether she'll stay married."

"I'm gonna get married in Las Vegas and honeymoon at Niagara Falls."

"Who's the lucky fella?"

Jennifer was silent, her eyes glued to the set. "The third man I come across on the next surf will be my first husband," she said and started whirling through the channels, both of them leaning forward. The first click was Tom Selleck.

"Eeew! Gross!" They both acted like they were puking.

The next channel was Johnny Depp on a *Jump Street* rerun. "Oh shit! Why can't he be number three?" Jennifer complained.

Courtney laughed. "He's saving himself for me."

The next channel was RuPaul.

"There ya go!" Courtney laughed.

"He doesn't count!" Jennifer protested.

The next channel was Heather Locklear on *Melrose Place.* She paused.

"I know who you're waiting for, you can't linger, surf!" Courtney whistled like a referee.

Jennifer went ahead, *Baywatch,* she paused again.

"Jennifer!" Courtney pushed her leg. Jennifer sped through the channels. Nature, car commercial, wrestling.

"There he is, that's him!" Courtney pointed, cracking up. "Wild Boy Rick and his All-Star Dick!" She laughed harder.

"No way! It's not fair." Jennifer stared at the screen. "I want Johnny Depp!"

Courtney went into the bathroom, poured herself a glass of water, came back, and lay down. She dug her nails into the bedspread, pulled it up to her chin, curled under it. "It's fucking freezing in here. Why is the air-conditioning on?"

"We have to get our money's worth."

Courtney curled farther down under the bedspread. "I thought you were going to marry David?"

Jennifer laughed. "David's too uncentered. He doesn't even have a job. His idea of making money is buying a book at a thrift store for fifty cents so he can sell it at Powell's for a dollar, then brag all day how he doubled his money. I don't want to marry a guy whose idea of transportation is a skateboard."

"So he's got a few hang-ups, look who's talking."

"It's just too awkward. He thinks the world is divided into two kinds of people, those who wear Converse All-Stars and those who don't. And I don't like any of his films, they're so pretentious." She sipped her beer. "Have you ever slept with him?"

"He treated me like a sister," Courtney said, leaning up, "asking advice about other women, then bringing them home, fucking them in the next room. He's like you, chasing something he can't have."

"Robert wants me, he just doesn't know how to show it."

"You mean physically?"

"What else would I be talking about?"

"Doesn't that sort of tip you off?" Courtney waved her hands in circular motions, as if to speed comprehension.

"Why should it? Sex is so eighties."

"What?"

"You know, with AIDS and stuff. It's a suicide trip."

"But hasn't it always been? I thought that was half the attraction?"

"For you maybe."

"You got any aspirin?" Courtney rubbed her forehead.

"I can do better than that." Jennifer set her Heineken on the nightstand, leaned over the side of her bed, and picked up her bag, pouring its contents onto the bed: hairbrush, address book, plane tickets, four or five orange prescription bottles.

"Welcome to happy world." Jennifer sorted the containers, found the bottle she wanted, cracked open the white childproof seal, popped two capsules as if she were swallowing vitamins, took a hit of her beer, killed it, tossed the can toward the wastebasket, missed, burped, started surfing again, the TV now a collage of shredded phrases as Jennifer intensified her search for a husband. Courtney looked at the label on one of the bottles.

"The blue ones are good," Jennifer said.

Courtney swallowed a blue one, reached for her water glass, sipped the edge, staring at the television screen.

"Remember the first time we got stoned?" Jennifer asked.

"Not really," Courtney said.

"We were in my bedroom after school, my mom came home and we got totally paranoid, so you smothered the room with Lysol and that made it stink even worse." Jennifer started cracking up. "Whenever I smell Lysol, I think of you."

"Gee thanks." Courtney set down her glass, stood and went into the bathroom, turned on the shower and undressed, letting the bathroom fill with steam. Sitting on the edge of the wide tub, she rubbed the muscles on the underside of her calves, examined the bruise on her thigh, the scrapes on both of her knees. She stood and pulled back the clear plastic curtain and stepped into the shower, soaped her hair and rinsed, thought about Bobby lying on his futon in the freezing squat, of Tommy pacing his flat full of bugs, of the wormy creep who raped her in the truck. A shiver ran through her, she leaned deeper under the hot water, scrubbing her armpits and between her legs, then checking her pubic hair for bugs. She turned off the water, stepped out of the tub, and wrapped herself in a large white towel. She stood beside the sink, found Jennifer's toothbrush and some toothpaste, wiping steam from the mirror with her other hand.

"Mirror mirror on the wall," she recited, "who's the fairest of them all?" She turned off the water, waited for a response, then spit into the sink.

Portland

We rolled down I-5 past Salem, Eugene, and Roseburg, nonstop until Grants Pass, a town of pickup trucks and Klansmen, a cluster of shopping malls clinging to the highway. Mary pulled into a twenty-four-hour truck stop. Two hunters in camouflage were parked ahead of us, their red van bearing a SOLDIERS FOR CHRIST bumper sticker. I went into the store and bought a six-pack of Heineken. The lady behind the counter wore an orange polyester smock and chewed gum like someone dying for a smoke. She looked me over, took my money, asked if I was from Portland. I nodded. End of conversation.

Mary went to the bathroom, seeing her walk off made me horny again, her little hips had a lazy sway that said *fuck me*. One of the guys in the van whistled at her, she ignored him. The truck stop was jammed, eighteen-wheelers parked side by side. Hungry cowboys burning on speed filled every booth of the restaurant, one eye on the runny eggs sliding off their forks and one eye on the skinny legs of the teenage waitress working behind the counter.

The attendant took the nozzle from the pump and started filling the tank. I paid for ten dollars worth of gas. Mary snuck up behind me, tickled my waist, scared the shit out of me, took the Heinekens, and got back into the car.

"I love the smell of gasoline," she said. The orange and red lights of semitrailers glowed like a carnival at closing time, a long stretch of mist crept over the soybean fields, a flatbed truck full of migrant workers sped past. Mary was revving the engine in true redneck fashion. I jumped back in, cracked a beer, pressed my feet against the dashboard. Mary swerved out of the lot.

As we sped through the forest, lightning flashed over the valley, illuminating the distant purple mountains. Flying away from roadkill in the center of the highway, a huge white owl with a fat piece of red flesh hanging from its beak floated over the windshield then banked into the black trees. I tried rolling a cigarette unsuccessfully, settled for a roach in the ashtray instead.

"So tell me about Phil," Mary said, changing lanes to pass an old VW van struggling through the first mountain pass.

"I've known him since high school. We moved out here together. He joined a fire crew a few months after we arrived and hasn't been back much since. He hangs out in the woods pretty much by himself."

"How does somebody become such a recluse?"

"A friend of ours was shot and killed. We were both in the car when it happened. Phil was really freaked. I don't think he ever got over it. Being out here, growing weed, maybe it's all he can handle."

"Who shot your friend?"

"The cops."

"Why?"

"Gary shot at them first." I pushed my empty beer bottle under the seat. "He had a little problem with authority."

"I guess."

"If that hadn't happened something else would have, he was a crazy motherfucker." I reached over and touched Mary's hair. "I loved him, but I don't miss him." The car got all quiet, a cold blank stare spread over Mary's face as she worked her way through my memories, or maybe sifted through her own. She passed another car, a rusted-out rice cooker sputtering up the hill.

"So what about this drug business, you guys make good money?"

"Enough to survive. I only sell it to friends, it disappears overnight. People are always calling to find out when I'll

have more. I'm not rich, but I don't have to work if that's
what you mean."

Rain started to fall, lightning crisscrossed over the tree
line, the windshield wipers took long lazy swipes over the
glass. Mary nursed her beer, I took another from the cooler
in the backseat, rolled up my flannel shirt, and used it as a
pillow.

"So how long have you been doing this?"

"Since we moved out here. Phil is the last of a dying
breed, most growers have moved indoors to hydroponics
and halogen bulbs."

"Why don't you guys grow indoors?"

"Too risky. The police monitor electric bills, one guy I
knew had a fire. If the cops come, you're busted, ten years
in the slammer. Out here, we're just innocent campers
caught in an FBI raid. They can't prove anything. Transportation and sales are the only risk."

"Oh great!" Mary said, wiping beer from her lips.

"Don't worry, your car is too loud to be suspicious, and
even if we did get pulled over, when was the last time a cop
tore apart your car in search of dope?"

We passed through Wilderville and Wonder following
Route 199, a pitch-black two-lane road lit only by moonlight
and orange reflectors, a long black stretch of old forest
highway that followed the riverbed. Selma was a patch of
light at the edge of the woods, a town without an intersec-
tion. Phil was sitting beside an abandoned gas pump outside the tiny grocery store.

"He's cute," Mary said, skidding across the gravel lot.

Phil's long blond hair hung on both sides of his face like curtains. He looked skinnier, in need of a shave, wearing green army pants, a blue and white flannel shirt, and black Converse All-Stars.

"I've been waitin' for hours," he said. We hugged. Mary grabbed a bottle of Wild Turkey that I'd stashed in the cooler, handed it to Phil.

"Hi, I'm Mary." She giggled.

Phil cracked open the bottle, took a big swig, wiped his mouth on his flannel shirt, then kissed her on both cheeks. I threw his pack in the trunk.

"Careful," he said, "those are my groceries."

We got into the car, all three in the front seat, and Phil guided us down a muddy gravel fire-road which bent downhill between thick weeds and tall stands of Douglas fir.

"Go slow," he said, "you never know what might be out here."

"It's so dark," Mary said, "I feel like I'm going to drive off the edge of the world."

We crawled down the muddy logging road some four or five miles, into the Kalmiopsis Wilderness near the base of Pearsoll Peak. Bugs raced toward the headlights, a cloud of dust billowed behind us. Mary leaned forward trying to anticipate the course, holding the steering wheel with both hands. Phil leaned forward as well, squinting through the glass. I took a swig from the Wild Turkey.

"Stop!" Phil yelled, grabbing Mary. "Turn off the lights."

Mary slowed down, hit the lights. Phil leaned toward me.

"Roll down your window."

"What? What is it?" I asked, rolling down the window.

"See that?"

"No."

"A spotter plane looking for campfires."

A small plane skimmed the tree line a mile ahead of us, then swayed left between two mountains and disappeared.

"He's following the riverbed. It's harvest season. The woods are red-hot." He squinted through the windshield. "OK, go ahead."

Mary turned the lights back on and lurched the car forward.

"Lots of Feds this season?"

"Ever known a man to fish at high noon?"

"Kinda obvious, huh?"

"Kinda, but they're more paranoid than we are, afraid of getting shot at by some crazy miner. So they come in numbers, not so much concerned with arrests as burning crops. People here have caught on, doing smaller plots spread over greater distances." Phil leaned over the dashboard. "It's just ahead now. There, over there, go ahead and park under that tree."

Mary stopped under an evergreen and we all piled out. It was so quiet everyone spoke in whispers, the absolute blackness was astounding. Without Phil's flashlight I wouldn't have been able to see my hand in front of my face. The terrain was hilly and I could hear the river to the left of us, twice I walked into low branches. Phil lived in an old miner's shack made of small trees and sheet metal that stood haphazardly beside the Illinois River. The dirt floor slanted toward the water, there was a woodstove and lawn chairs. Mary sat on a log.

"A mule carried this stove out here over a hundred years ago," Phil said, lighting a match to newspaper, sticking it under some kindling. "Some miner built this shack around it."

The woods were alive with strange sounds, Mary kept clutching my arm whenever a certain owl called out.

"The air smells like juniper," she said. "It makes me sleepy." She leaned against my arm and closed her eyes. The woodstove's orange glow filled the room. There were wooden shelves on one wall filled with tin cans, a stack of plastic buckets and hoses pushed into the corner, a large air mattress leaning against the wall.

"How's your crop?" I asked.

"You tell me." Phil rolled a fat joint on his purple Frisbee, then handed it to me.

I lit it, took a hit, and started coughing, the rich sweet smoke expanded in my lungs. Phil laughed. I passed it to Mary, she took a hit, started coughing too.

"That's some serious boo." I rubbed my eyes.

"You guys must be tired after that long drive." Phil took a hit, passed it back to me.

"Mary drove the whole way," I said and tried another toke, coughed again and passed it to Mary. She passed it to Phil. He put it out. We all spaced out, silent, listening to the fire crackle and the water tear over the riverbed.

"Mary can have the air mattress," Phil said. "You and I will have to rough it on the ground, but we can share the mattress as a pillow."

Phil handed me a wool blanket, keeping the down sleeping bag for himself. Watching the fire slowly turn to coals and burn itself out, I kept feeling bugs crawling on me, but every time I brushed them away, there was nothing.

When I woke, Mary was off the mattress and curled against me, the sun was bright, and Phil was gone. I sat up and peered between the warped planks that made up the wall. Phil was slicing apples into a bowl, he already had a small fire burning. The shack looked better at night. There were mouse turds beside the air mattress, flies circling overhead, the sleeping bag was covered with a fine layer of honey-colored soil. Freezing, I went out and knelt beside the fire, warmed my hands against the flames.

"That's a beautiful woman you've found," Phil said. "You don't want to sell her, do ya?"

"Nah."

"What happened to Courtney?"

"She burned down the house and ran off to New York."

"Say what?"

"When I got there, the place was a giant bonfire, it was gone in minutes. I saved a piece of melted glass for ya."

"Oh man." Phil shook his head, pacing around the fire. "What a bummer. I knew that chick was bad news. Always mumbling to herself, using kindling to draw symbols in the dirt, all that witchiepoo stuff. Man, I'm telling you, she was weird."

"I'm crashing at Robert and Tony's until I can get a new place."

"Oh man, double bummer. You aren't turning into one of them, are ya? I mean, it's OK if you are, it's just . . ."

"No, I'm not queer. They're the only people I know with an extra bedroom, that's all. The place is like a twenty-four-hour party palace, I don't get much sleep."

"Listen, if you want, you can move down here for a while."

"Nah, I think I'm better off up there. I mean, I have to start over sooner or later."

"Well, she's a fresh start," he whispered, pointing toward the cabin.

"Good morning," Mary said sleepily, walking toward us, the sleeping bag wrapped over her shoulders.

"Sleep OK?" Phil asked, pouring granola into wooden bowls.

"The ground was a little hard, but I managed."

"Coffee will be ready in a minute, have some cereal." Phil handed her a bowl of granola.

Mary was shivering, but looked extremely sexy surrounded by nature. Her skin was flushed, her paisley-shaped eyes glowing in the crisp morning light, her hair matted like tangled ribbons after a birthday party. I noticed Phil staring.

"You all ready for a swim?" he asked.

"Not until after coffee," Mary protested. "Is the pool heated?"

"Warm as Mother Nature can make it," he said.

"That doesn't sound very promising," she said.

"There's some hot springs," he promised. "In the right spot it's like a warm bath in the Garden of Eden."

Mary clutched her coffee cup, shivered, rubbed her hands together. "I don't think so." She leaned closer to the fire.

The smell of wood smoke and wet leaves hovered over the campsite. The air was damp, but the chill I had when I first woke up was gone. Mary smiled at me, she looked happy. Phil refilled our cups.

After breakfast we followed Phil up a spruce-needle path surrounded by wild daisies and marionberry bushes to a small ridge overlooking the water. He took off his clothes and jumped into the river, swimming toward the warm spot. Mary looked back at me, blushed, then stripped off all her clothes.

"No shame?"

"Are you kidding?" She smiled. "I'm a professional," she said, and jumped in. She surfaced screaming. "It's so cold!" Then started splashing me.

"C'mon." She waved, floating toward Phil.

I undressed and dove off, surfacing beside Mary, her soft body slippery and smooth like an ice cube floating in a vodka tonic. She grabbed my shoulders and kissed me, her tongue pressed between my lips, both of us sinking into the stream.

"I feel like Adam and Eve." She pushed away and floated on her back.

"Then who's that guy?" I said, pointing at Phil kicking against the current.

"The devil," she said. "And soon we'll be cast out of this

paradise, back into the bowels of Portland, don't you get it? It's so lyrical, a man who leaves his natural state lives with darkness forever."

Mary broke off, swam toward the steamy edge of the water where the hot springs bubbled below the river. I followed her, watching her bare ass skim the surface of the water. She stopped a few yards from Phil and waited for me, treading water. Phil was settled in a small pool he'd made with a circle of rocks, eyes closed, head tilted toward the sun.

"I've never felt so clean," Mary said, her voice shaking from the cold.

"Me too," I lied. She kissed me and I sank under the water, the river's current pulling me away from the warm spot. I could see huge trout swimming over the moss-covered rocks, the water was so clear. There seemed to be a hazy magic in the trees, the sun warmed my eyelids.

Mary climbed out first, squeezing water from her long black hair. A thin strand of multicolored beads hung between her breasts. I looked over at Phil. He cracked a huge smile.

After our swim Phil made a small fire, boiled some water, made another round of coffee. Mary and I warmed our palms around the smokey flames.

"Should we take a hike?" Phil asked. "It'll warm you up." He rubbed Mary's shoulders. She nodded. "I'll show you my strawberry patch."

We stashed the cooking gear in the shed, then climbed

a steep hill through thorny blackberry bushes to a crest, then followed a deer trail to a ridge overlooking the next valley. His plants were in a cliff side alcove, camouflaged from the air by army surplus netting hanging tree to tree, high enough to catch eight hours of sunshine. Some plants were seven feet tall with stalks thick as baseball bats, the leaves larger than my head, the buds purple and sticky, the size of carrots. The whole forest reeked of ganja.

Phil dug up a stash sealed in plastic under a rock and some leaves, concealed in a bed of ghost fern and nettle. I handed him some papers and he rolled a Magic-Marker-sized doobie.

Lying on a large white rock overlooking the hillside hemlock, we soaked up some afternoon sun, smoking reefer until stoned silent. Mary fell asleep. I sat beside Phil, watching puffy clouds engulf one another high above the scraggy peaks of the Coast Range. Shrilling birdcalls and the rhythmic buzz of insects pulsed in the background, the air smelled of winter rot baking in the hot sun.

"How's it been going out here?" I asked. "Don't you ever get lonely?"

"Time passes real slow, there's a lot of time," he said, staring into the sky. I looked over at him and wondered whether he would ever come back to civilization, and whether I would ever leave.

"Don't you miss the six o'clock news?" I asked.

He looked at me like I was an asshole. "Hell no." Shifting his weight, he pointed at a clear-cut across the valley, a hillside of tree stumps. "See that? There's your fucking six o'clock news."

NewYork

Courtney woke, pushed aside her blankets, climbed out of the king size bed, wrapped herself in a white towel.

Jennifer was still asleep. Courtney took the room key, turned off the light, and closed the door, slipped a DO NOT DISTURB tag on the door handle, then went down the hotel corridor in search of a Coke machine. Passing one, two, three hallways and then a balcony overlooking the massive lobby, she tried to imagine how many people had fucked in this building. She clutched the brass banister and leaned over the railing. There was an endless amount of doors, like a science fiction movie.

A half-eaten croissant sat on a silver breakfast tray outside a door marked DO NOT DISTURB. Starving, she grabbed it and put it in her mouth, sucked on the buttery flakes. Across the corridor she noticed several open rooms where maids were cleaning. She sauntered over to one, squeezed by the towel cart, and walked in. The maid didn't hear her, the vacuum was on. Courtney slipped into the bathroom and locked the door. On the counter was a blue bottle of perfume. She picked it up, then sprayed under her armpits, across her neck and tummy. Hanging over the shower rod were several pairs of nylons, she pulled down the black thigh-highs and slipped them on under her towel. Slowly she cracked open the bathroom door, hesitated, checked for the maid, then walked into the room. The maid noticed her and was startled, somewhat embarrassed, started apologizing in some Asian language. Courtney opened the closet and smiled, reached for the solid black mini with gold buttons. Letting the towel fall off her body, she dressed quickly in front of the maid, who turned away embarrassed and refolded some sheets. Courtney fastened the black satin belt and tried on the shoes—too small. She bowed toward the maid and quickly left the room, ran down the hall to Jennifer's room, quietly entered, and sat on the edge of the bed to lace up her Doc Martens. Jennifer awoke.

"Courtney, what time is it? Where'd you get that outfit?" she asked, rubbing her eyes.

"Goodwill," Courtney said, looking through Jennifer's makeup bag. On top were the little orange prescription bottles, Courtney read the labels—Benzedrine, Methedrine, Caffedrine—she had all the drines.

"Isn't that a Chanel suit?" She reached over and felt the material.

"I don't know," Courtney said, using Jennifer's red lipstick. Jennifer crawled out of bed and went into the bathroom.

"My head is throbbing," Courtney said, "do you have any aspirin?"

"In my purse," Jennifer yelled from behind the door.

Courtney rifled through Jennifer's purse and grabbed a twenty.

"I have to go over to my loft real quick and get a few things," she said. "I'll be right back."

"I want to come too!" Jennifer yelled from behind the door.

"We don't have time, we'll miss our flight. I'll be right back." Courtney turned and slammed the door.

She rode down the glass elevator, went outside, waved down a cab, and jumped into the backseat admiring the gold buttons of her new best friend. The streets rushed past like a rewinding video, she felt the tension in her neck already dissolving.

"There is no address on this building?" the driver asked.

"It's the big brown one with the cinder blocks in the windows." She pointed.

"This is your house?" he asked.

"No, it's my headquarters. I'm a terrorist." She smiled, handing him the twenty. He handed her the change suspiciously, using the little slot in the bulletproof glass. She stiffed him on the tip and slammed the door. The squat was barricaded, the entrance hole sealed with debris, empty shopping carts were tipped over the missing sidewalk.

"Bobby!" she screamed in front of the building. She hated doing this, but there was no other way.

"Bobby!" she yelled again.

The little Hispanic man on the corner started toward her.

"Hey lady, you change your mind or what? You want to go to my brother's place now?" he asked. She ignored him.

"Bobby!" she yelled.

"You wasting your time, lady," he said. "They all gone."

"Bobby!" she yelled with half the strength.

"You don't hear me? They gone."

"What?"

"The police clear the neighborhood, chase everybody out of the building. Nobody there no more."

"Fuck," she said. "Fuck. Where'd they go?" He shrugged his shoulders, pointed in three different directions.

Courtney walked toward Avenue A. The neighborhood was deserted, except for the usual early morning creepy crawlers sifting the pavement for bottles and cans, rummaging through bulging trash cans.

"That little shit is probably selling my stuff on St. Marks Place this very minute," she mumbled to herself, circling the block, walking all the way to Third Avenue. She raised her arm to stop a cab.

"Forty-eighth and Broadway," she said, getting into the car.

The cab started down the block, just then she spotted Bobby pushing a shopping cart filled with blankets, clothes, his books piled on top.

"Stop the car," she screamed. The car skidded. Courtney jumped out.

"Hey lady, your fare!" The driver pointed at the meter.

"Stay right there, asshole!" She slammed the door. The cab sped away. Courtney ran up behind Bobby.

"Hey man, where the hell's my stuff?" she asked.

"The cops took it," Bobby said, as if he were expecting her.

"Liar!" she screamed.

"They did! They said it was evidence." He shrugged, threw his arms out in innocence.

"How come you got your stuff then?" She pushed the cart.

"Because I was there to get it. Where were you, out fucking Donald Trump?" His eyes ran over her suit jacket.

"No I wasn't, shithead." She knelt down to lace her Doc Martens.

"Fucking slut," he mumbled and turned away.

"Get a life, Bobby!" She trailed him.

"No, Courtney." He spun around and pointed. "You get a life."

"Loser!" she screamed.

"Sell out!" he yelled back.

Courtney turned and flagged down another cab. She jumped in back and the cab bounced uptown.

"Fuckin' A." She made a fist and pressed it against her lips. "Everything gone. Clothes. Diary. Phone numbers."

"You talking to me?" the cabbie asked.

"Every time I leave town God swoops down and steals back the little progress I've made, every tiny gain is taken away." She hugged her legs, pressed them against her breast, tucked her chin between her knees.

"Maybe you should get a new God?" The cabbie stared into his rearview mirror.

Courtney pulled her skirt down, crossed her legs, glanced at her fingers, there was dirt under the nails. The cab stopped outside the hotel, she paid, then went in the back way, rode up the freight elevator, then quickly walked to Jennifer's room and slammed the door. Jennifer was packed, sitting in front of MTV.

"Where have you been?" Jennifer sat up.

"There were some complications."

"Where's your luggage? Did you leave it downstairs?"

"I'm having it sent."

"Huh?"

"I didn't have time to pack. My roommate's gonna do it for me and send a box UPS. She has an account at work, so it's cool."

Jennifer looked at her suspiciously.

"C'mon, we're outta here."

Outside the hotel the last yellow leaves clung to the fingers of trees, paper scraps spun in spirals over the cold autumn square. Courtney stretched, rubbed her bloodshot eyes.

"Let's get some breakfast," Courtney said, "there's a

diner across the street." She pointed. They ran across the street, dodging cabs, Jennifer lugging her bag. Courtney pulled open the glass door and they slid into opposite sides of a red vinyl booth. A strange plastic flower stood in a slender white vase, old ketchup stains stuck on the yellow petals.

"Would you like some coffee?" the waitress asked.

Courtney looked up and saw a very beautiful woman blushing.

"Two please," she said.

"And a toasted cinnamon-raisin bagel," Jennifer added.

The waitress smiled and walked away.

"I'll bet she hasn't been in this city more than two days," Courtney said, "too friendly, too happy, there aren't any circles under her eyes. She doesn't have that gray city pallor, when your face looks like a sidewalk."

Jennifer watched her disappear, slouched in her seat, and gazed out the window.

"That's the problem with New York," Courtney continued, "even the most awesome babes end up being waitresses."

"Maybe she's an actress between jobs," Jennifer said hopefully.

"Right. And I'm a supermodel flying off to Paris."

"Are you nervous?" Jennifer asked. "Your pupils are dilated."

"I hate to fly."

The order bell rang, Courtney glanced outside. The street was crowded, people merging from one place to another. They all seemed familiar in their unfamiliarity. Court-

ney looked at her reflection in a spoon, as if she were
holding a mirror.

The waitress set their cups and Jennifer's bagel on the
table. The order bell rang.

"I'm so glad you're moving back to Portland," Jennifer
said, spreading the melted butter on her bagel with a knife.

"I'm not moving, it's only a visit, I didn't say I'd stay. I
thought you were moving to New York?"

"New York seems a bit stressed out right now," Jennifer
said.

"Did you get any souvenirs?" Courtney asked, sipping
her coffee.

"No."

"We'll look for some empty crack vials on the way to the
airport." Jennifer bit into her bagel, stared at two women
kissing good-bye on the street corner. Holding hands, the
shorter one lingered, not wanting to let go.

"Have you ever made out with a girl?" Jennifer asked.

"No, why, you?"

"No, but I always wondered what it would be like,"
Jennifer said. "I just love the way women smell."

"Maybe you should be the perfume girl at Nordstrom's?"

"Women are softer, more approachable, maybe that's
why I find Robert so attractive. He's so delicate, so un-
macho."

"Kinda makes you wonder, doesn't it?"

"About what?"

"Never mind." Courtney took a bite out of Jennifer's
bagel. "The way I see it," she said with her mouth full of
food, "you put a quarter in the gum-ball machine hoping to

get a watch, but sometimes you end up with neon shoe-
laces. Someday I'll settle down and marry a rock star."

Jennifer swallowed the last bite of her bagel.

"C'mon, let's go," she said, "or we'll miss our plane."

Courtney left the waitress her last dollar bill.

A taxicab idled at the curb, a Middle Eastern melody
blasting. Drivers trapped in gridlock started blaring their
horns. Courtney glanced into the sky, gray and white clouds
hovered over the canyon of glass skyscrapers. She saw a
man in the third-floor window of an office tower working a
copier machine, his face glowing in the bright green light.
Boarding the silver bus headed for the airport, she
crouched in a window seat, remembered a box of old
photographs she'd stored at Bobby's, a collection of post-
cards, letters from old friends. Specific pictures came to
mind: herself as a small child wearing a Batgirl sweatshirt,
her mother in front of the hospital feeding ducks, David
naked in the bathtub, flipping her the bird.

The bus started up, turned down Forty-second Street,
then again at First Avenue, then rumbled into the Midtown
Tunnel. Potholes gutted the road and the bus seemed to hit
every one. A pinkish gray wad of hard gum was stuck to the
window ledge and an odd stale smell lingered in the seats,
she couldn't help thinking it was cum.

"This scenery will never make it on a postcard," Jennifer
said as the bus emerged from the tunnel in Queens and
sped down the Long Island Expressway. "It's so ugly, why
doesn't anyone pick up all the garbage?"

Courtney didn't answer. Unable to focus, she saw the scenery speeding away like a grainy silent film, her breath frosting the window.

The bus stopped outside the terminal. Jennifer retrieved her luggage from the storage area under the bus. Courtney followed her through the electronic doors of the terminal. The airport was solid white, plotted like a space station. When they checked in, Courtney insisted on a window seat toward the front.

"People always die in the back," Courtney said.

"What are you talking about?" Jennifer asked.

"When the plane crashes." Courtney made a face like Jennifer was an imbecile.

They went through the metal detectors and waited at the gate for the plane to start boarding. Jennifer leafed through *Elle* magazine, Courtney sat in a TV chair overlooking the runway. Loudspeaker voices announced departing flights. The thought of being on a plane for five hours made her nauseous.

"Courtney, you don't look so good, are you OK?" Jennifer asked. Courtney's jaw quivered, her lips got shaky, she felt herself about to cry, forced a smile. Jennifer closed her magazine.

"You can always come back." She hugged her.

"I don't want to come back," Courtney replied. "I hate New York." She felt her stomach knot twist tighter, sensed a migraine coming on, patted her pockets in search of a cigarette.

"It's not your fault, most of it has to do with luck, being in the right place at the right time."

"I'm always in the wrong place at the wrong time."

"You always have another chance."

Courtney laughed, rubbed the corner of her eye.

"What's so funny?"

"Nothing, I just can't believe you're the one telling me this. C'mon, I don't want to miss our plane." Courtney stood.

"Wait, I want some gum," Jennifer said.

"Hurry up."

Courtney looked at the life-insurance booth, thought about buying five dollars worth, then realized she would never collect.

They handed over their tickets and descended through the mobile hallway, the last to get on the plane. Courtney latched her seat belt as the plane taxied away from the gate and got in line for the runway. Courtney squirmed in her seat, already uncomfortable. When they finally sped down the runway and lifted from the ground, Courtney clutched Jennifer's hand, felt sweat trickle under her arm.

"Do you smell that?" Jennifer asked.

"What!?" Courtney looked out the window to see if the engine was on fire. "Smoke?"

"It smells like plastic in here," Jennifer complained. "I feel like I'm in a tube of toothpaste."

"Look out there," Courtney said, "something's on fire."

"That's the ozone layer or whatever they call it, it's supposed to be all brown."

The plane rose higher over New Jersey, oil tanks covered the seaboard, the residue of slender factory smokestacks drifted toward the Atlantic Ocean.

"They look like tiny pills," Courtney said, pointing to the refinery storage facilities. "The swamps beside them look like they're filled with puss."

The seat-belt sign went off, but they both kept theirs on. Courtney leaned forward, took out the plastic emergency flyer and the barf bag.

"Say there's an explosion, right? And we're blown to smithereens, do body parts just fall out of the sky?"

"Courtney, please," Jennifer said, setting down her magazine. "Planes only crash when they take off and land, they don't blow up in midair."

"What about that one in Scotland with all the schoolgirls inside?"

"That was terrorism, that's different. There aren't any terrorists in the skies over Pennsylvania."

"I guess you're right." Courtney looked out the small plastic window, leaned forward to look back at New York City.

The plane lifted over the clouds and the horizon came into view. Jennifer leaned over Courtney's lap to get a look.

"This is like the viewpoint of God," Jennifer said.

"Don't say that," Courtney said.

"Why?"

"Because I don't see any people down there."

Portland

Tramping through the woods, Phil led and I followed Mary up a steep narrow path, past a waterfall surrounded by maidenhair ferns and an old cave with strange markings on the black stone. Huge fallen trees covered with moss and orange shelf mushrooms crisscrossed over the rocks of the stream above the falls. Salamanders and chipmunks whipped across the trail, birds shuttered through the dark branches above, Mary's little ass swayed in her skintight jeans, working the path in cork-heel sandals.

"Slow down," I pleaded, but she pretended not to hear, intoxicated by the sweet moist air, the sound of rushing water. Phil paused at the peak of the trail beside a massive Douglas fir. Red-capped mushrooms sprouted at its base, smothered by lacy spiderwebs. Looking across the valley, the foliage seemed prehistoric, as if evolution hadn't quite caught up here yet.

"Are there any Indians out here?" Mary turned and asked.

"No, they've all been put into concentration camps in the desert," Phil said.

"That's sad." Mary lay down on a pile of brown leaves in a sun-worshiping position, her long legs stretching away from her waist. I thought about the Indians, wondered if all the violence in America wasn't a curse, or worse, if what we did to the Native Americans was only a precursor of what we would do to ourselves.

We sat quietly, resting from the walk. Phil foraged around the bushes, collecting blackberries in a small brown paper bag. Being with him reminded me of the time we drove up to Mt. St. Helens after the eruption. The logging roads were covered with a foot of ash packed down by emergency equipment. His Ford Falcon rode like a dune buggy along the still-swollen banks of the Toutle River. We saw a herd of elk run across the road, up a hillside, jumping over three-hundred-year-old trees blown over as if a giant comb had groomed the mountains. As far as the eye could see, trees, side by side like matchsticks, all of it buried in light gray volcanic ash. We parked beside a scorched Toyota. Phil got in the driver's seat to pose for a picture. A little yellow tag was tied onto the aerial antenna, flapping in the wind.

When Phil and I climbed up a rocky hillside to get a view of Spirit Lake, a tremor shook the ground and suddenly the earth shifted left to right. I lost my footing and slid down the jagged stone-faced cliff, grabbing a small evergreen stump on the way down to stop my free fall. My camera went ahead of me and smashed on the rocks a hundred feet below. My ankle was sprained, my arms all scraped up. Phil climbed over and helped me down off the cliff. I remember waiting for him, my chin resting on that cold rock, thinking that if I ever made it down, I would never enter the woods again.

Mary got up and picked a batch of wildflowers, a silent message that it was time to go.

"Aren't these the most beautiful flowers you've ever seen?" she asked, arranging them by color. She pulled a petal off a white daisy.

"He loves me," she said, then pulled another, "he loves me not."

I kissed her, the flowers were crushed between us.

Phil came out of the woods with a big plastic garbage bag. "Here's something to keep you going." He handed it to Mary. "I'll trade you for the cooler in your trunk and everything inside it."

Mary opened the big plastic bag, looked over at me. "It's a deal," she said.

Phil led us away from the campsite on a different path, or maybe it was the same one. There were footprints headed in both directions. We came out of the woods beside Mary's car, wet leaves were clinging to the hood. Mary opened the trunk, gave Phil the cooler.

"We'll hook up soon." Phil gave me a hug. "I need to come up to Portland for an Earth First benefit." Mary kissed him twice. He picked up the cooler and disappeared into the trees.

Mary warmed up the car while I pulled out the backseat and stashed the weed. She lit two cigarettes, handed me one, then backed out from under the tree.

As we sailed toward the interstate, the dense woods thinned out, became low-lying trees, then flat land covered with sagebrush, then squat warehouses with telephone wire strung post to post.

"I get the feeling you hate to leave," Mary said.

"Sometimes I worry about him, out there, all alone. I wonder what he's thinking."

"I'm sure he's thinking the same about you," she said. Somehow that made me feel better. We passed a caravan of Winnebagos. A small child peered out a back window and waved to us. I waved back, leaned against Mary, put one hand under her thigh between the vinyl seat and her jeans.

"If we get caught, I'm gonna kill you," she said.

"And if we don't?"

"I might anyway."

I rubbed her thigh. "Relax, baby. We're already home free." I had to loosen her up, she was getting nervous, making me jumpy as well.

"What was your first sexual experience?" I asked.

"Meeting you, of course," she said.

"No, before that."

"Oh God, let's see." She paused. "Well, when I was in junior high school we had a neighbor, a tall Jewish guy, who bought us beer on the weekends. One day he invited me and my girlfriends over to his place to party. He dared us to take off all our clothes, of course we refused. 'Show us your dick,' my girlfriend blurted out, and of course he did. It was so huge and hairy and not at all what I imagined. We were thoroughly grossed out, and begged him to put it away. He offered us money to touch it, but we refused. He offered us a dollar for every time we could hit his cock with a lit match from a distance. This we agreed to. He pulled his pants down to his ankles and we flicked matches toward his erection. When his pubic hair ignited, he started batting out the flames with his hand. We all cracked up, it was so fucking hilarious. From then on I couldn't stop thinking about boys."

"You were thinking about boys in the seventh grade?"

"Every girl does, what's so weird about that?" she said. "I used to ride my bike to Little League games and circle the fields, checking out the boys. When I was old enough, I joined and played shortstop. After the games the whole team went out for ice cream. I was surrounded by boys."

"You played shortstop?"

"I was a tomboy, I used to beat the shit out of my brother and his friends, feel that muscle," she said.

I leaned over and felt her flexed arm, reached down and felt her breast. She squirmed, the car swerved across the highway, Mary steadied it in the other lane.

"Keep your cock in your pants or we'll do a James Dean," she said.

I fiddled with the radio dial, found a country western

station, Patsy Cline sang, I thought about the movie, when the plane crashed, wondered if all my coolest memories were from television.

"What about you?" she asked. "Who was your first love? Did you have a burning crush on Marcia Brady? Tell the truth."

"It happened in Little League," I said.

"Make it with the batgirl?" she asked.

"No, one of the player's moms."

Mary coughed up her beer, it squirted out of her nose, she was laughing so hard.

"It's true," I said, trying not to crack a smile. "I met a boy on the team with long brown hair, his name was Chelsea, he was the pitcher. We rode our bikes home in the same direction, so we became friends. One night he took me to the Catholic school fair. We cruised the promenade together, looking for girls without their parents. His mother was divorced. She worked nights as a waitress and always came home late. After the fair, we went over to his house, sipped a little of his mother's liquor stash, smoked some cigarettes. To make a long story short, she walked in on us.

" 'What are you doing?' she yelled. 'How dare you?' Pulling the cigarette from my hand she extinguished it in a large star-shaped Hollywood ashtray brimming with butts.

" 'Does your mother know you smoke?' she asked, waving the cigarette in front of my face. 'I'm sure she'd like to know.'

"I looked at Chelsea, really scared. She took off her jacket, threw down her bag, and sat between us.

" 'Where did you get the cigarettes?' she asked, lighting one herself.

" 'We found them,' I said, 'on the street.'

" 'And the brandy?' We were both silent.

" 'What am I going to do with you two?' She turned toward me.

" 'What's your phone number?' She picked up the phone. 'I'm going to have a chat with your father.' She stared at me.

" 'Please don't,' I said, but she reached for the phone, began dialing, then hung up. She unlaced her tennis shoes. I begged her not to call, said I would do anything.

"She locked Chelsea in his room, then pushed me into the bathroom and locked the door. She took off her clothes, told me to do the same. I was embarrassed and undressed slowly, fidgeted with the buttons. I had never seen a woman in the nude before. She turned on the shower water, then squatted in front of me and unzipped my pants, pulled them down. She grabbed the back of my legs and kissed the bulge in my white underwear.

" 'Get in,' she said, 'and wash me, especially between my legs.'

"I kept my underwear on and stepped into the water, she followed. We stood facing one another in the shower. She pushed my face between her breasts and stroked my penis with a soapy hand, then pulled off my underwear and rinsed our bodies with a handheld nozzle.

" 'I don't think it's clean enough.' She pointed to her pussy. 'You'd better use your mouth.' She leaned against the tile, pushing my head between her legs."

"No way, that really happened?" Mary laughed.

"Nah, actually, I never got laid in high school. I read that in *Penthouse.*"

Portland

The plane descended slowly toward Portland International Airport, a thick layer of gray clouds hung over the Willamette Valley, all Courtney could see were the pointy snowcapped peaks of the Cascade Mountains, from Mt. Rainier to the Three Sisters east of Eugene.

"My socks already feel soggy." Courtney leaned on Jennifer's arm. "What are you reading?"

"An Edith Wharton novel," Jennifer said. Courtney shrugged, noticed a little white church on the cover.

"Looks boring," she grumbled, glancing up the aisle.

"Some guy in the novel wants to do the dirty with Mattie, it snows a lot, Mattie wears muffs," Jennifer replied flatly, her eyes glued to the text.

The stewardess came by asking everyone to put their seats in the upright position and to fasten their seat belts, make sure their tray tables were securely fastened. The plane tilted and the clouds broke, houses came into view. Courtney gripped her armrest tightly as the plane shook with turbulence descending through the clouds.

"Remember when we were little and that plane ran out of gas and crash-landed on Burnside?" Courtney asked, shaking Jennifer's arm.

"Courtney please, not now for heaven's sake."

The houses got larger and larger until Courtney could almost see inside the bedroom windows. They drifted out over the Columbia River and landed smoothly on the long strip of runway.

Jennifer led Courtney through the carpeted airport, past the photomural of Mt. Hood, through the sliding glass doors to an orange Tri-Met bus. Japanese tourists in bright-colored windbreakers blocked the entrance.

"Which way Twin Peaks?" the group leader asked.

Jennifer pushed her way through them.

"Please, no photos of Madonna. No photos." She shook her hand, yanking Courtney through the crowd. A flashbulb went off, followed by another.

"Madonna, Madonna," the tourists reassured one another, some bowing as Courtney and Jennifer stepped onto the bus. They took a seat all the way in the back.

"Very funny," Courtney said. "Very funny."

When the bus pulled away Courtney waved to the Japanese and another volley of flashbulbs exploded in her eyes.

They crossed the Willamette River, massive cranes were unloading vessels berthed along the waterfront. She couldn't read the fine print on the boxes, but the initials TV were unmistakable.

"Oh God, the memories are bursting in now," Courtney said, as the bus crawled through Old Town. "I don't dare walk these streets alone, who knows what closet door might fling open," she said, staring at clusters of people on the sidewalk, looking for someone familiar. "Portland is so small it makes me nervous," she said, itching the side of her face. "I know I'll be sucked right back in, life is too easy here, people aren't bothered enough, there's no tension."

"I'm sure you'll give everyone a reason to be tense," Jennifer said.

"Promise me I won't wake up in some stranger's apartment two weeks from now wondering why nobody loves me," Courtney pleaded.

"Everybody loves you, Courtney," Jennifer said. "You can have any boy you want."

"I want somebody to want me!" Courtney screamed. Everyone on the bus turned to stare. Jennifer blushed, looked out the window.

They got off at Morrison Street and walked up the park blocks to Jennifer's place, past the Masonic temple and the art museum. A NO SKATEBOARDING sign was attached to the Abe Lincoln statue. Pigeons pooped on his head, green streaks of rain-soaked copper ran over his face. Shopping-cart people filled the benches. One crazy old lady was talking to herself. Courtney couldn't help thinking about her mother as she stared at the old woman's swollen pink ankles.

Jennifer's apartment building had a heavy wooden door with blue glass windows, an old map of the Pacific Northwest was framed in the hallway. Jennifer fitted the key into the lock and pushed open the door of her apartment. She dropped her bags, rushed into the room. All the dresser drawers were pulled out, clothing was lying all over the place, as if the laundry basket had exploded.

"I think I've been robbed!" Jennifer screamed. She looked around, frenzied, going through everything to see what was missing.

"Are you a drug dealer?" Courtney asked calmly.

"No!"

"Does someone have a key? None of the windows were opened and the front door was locked," Courtney said, checking around. "They didn't take your boombox or CDs, guess they didn't like your taste in music."

"Courtney come here! Quick!" Jennifer yelled waving her arm frantically. "That's him, the psycho killer!" Jennifer pointed into the parking lot. "It must have been him! You're a witness, he's leaving the scene of the crime!" Jennifer was hysterical.

Courtney threw down the CD and went over to the window.

"Too much of a stoner to be a psycho killer, trust me, I know," Courtney said matter-of-factly.

"Then who did this?!" Jennifer yelled.

"Chill, your eyeballs are gonna pop out of your head, think a minute, who has the key?"

"Only Robert has my key," Jennifer said, "but he's never used it."

"And what's missing?" Courtney asked.

"My underwear! All of it! Gone!" Jennifer started screaming again.

"Please, you're gonna break my eardrums," Courtney begged. "There has to be a logical answer for this." Courtney went into the bathroom to pee.

"How can you go to the bathroom at a time like this?!" Jennifer pounded on the door. "He might come back any second!"

"I gotta go!" Courtney yelled from the other side of the door. Jennifer looked through the rest of her belongings.

"Shit!"

"What?" Courtney asked.

"He took my diary, too!"

"Did you write anything about me?" Courtney asked.

"You? Is that all you can think about? Some psycho killer is masturbating this very moment with my diary and underwear, and all you care about is whether I wrote about you?"

Courtney opened the door. "Well, did you?" she asked.

"Yes, of course."

"Great, that's fucking great. I come back to town and you set me up for murder!"

"Murder!?" Jennifer sat on the bed, suddenly quiet.

"Don't worry." Courtney pulled a long black object from her purse. "See this button?" Courtney pushed it, a switchblade popped out. "Any asshole who sneaks in here, I'll cut off his balls." Courtney waved the knife in the air.

"Where'd you get that?" Jennifer asked.

"At the airport," she said, "while you were in the bathroom. My first purchase in Oregon. C'mon, we're outta here."

Jennifer locked the door, double-checked the lock, then followed Courtney down the stairs.

"Let's start with Robert," Courtney said. "Does he live in the same place?"

"Yeah."

"Well, let's go over there."

"But I look like shit!"

"Maybe the sympathy factor will work for you, c'mon."

They walked over to Robert's place, past the Laundromat, the Plaid Pantry, and the Jefferson Theater.

"Does Sheila still make porn films?" Courtney asked.

"Yes," Jennifer said, "and practically everyone in town has been in one."

"Have you?" Courtney asked.

"Please," she sighed, "I'm worth more than a hundred dollars, thank you."

They walked down the hill to Robert's place, up the stairs of the sagging front porch, knocked on the front door.

"I think I hear a TV." Courtney opened the door. "Well slit my wrists," she said, seeing Tony and Robert dressed up in Jennifer's underwear watching television, an open bottle of Scotch on the TV tray placed between them. Robert looked up, obviously drunk, crunching ice between his teeth.

"Courtney?" Robert seemed surprised, Jennifer screamed.

Tony kicked his legs up on the footrest, stretching out a bra and panties. Robert was wearing white pajama bottoms with feet in them.

"What are you doing?!" Jennifer yelled. "Where did you get that?" She snapped the bra Tony was wearing. He shrieked like a little girl. "Did you assholes break into my apartment and steal all my underwear?"

Robert looked at Tony, Tony looked at Robert.

"Take it off! This instant! And where's my diary?"

Tony stood up. "Don't look," he said, acting coy, unlatching the tiny black bra stuffed with toilet paper.

Courtney went into the kitchen, opened the refrigerator, and took out a beer. "Am I Sherlock fucking Holmes or what?" she said.

Part Three

Portland

Hail rattled the roof of Mary's car, the defroster roared, the windshield wipers flapped back and forth at high speed, but the view was still a murky blur. I leaned into the back, pulled the seat cushion out, grabbed the pot, then wedged the seat back into place. Mary tugged my shirt, gave me a long mushy kiss. Her lips were dry and she smelled of wet soil.

"I'll probably have to work late tonight," she said, her voice slow with exhaustion. "Stop by for a drink later."

I kissed her again, squeezed the soft flesh above her knee, leaned against the door, hesitated, then jumped out and ran for the house. Mary beeped and drove away.

Upstairs, Robert and Tony were getting ready for another night at the Wild West. Tony, wearing a starched white nurse's uniform and a miniature white cap, was sitting on the couch, paging through *Vogue* magazine, gasping at supermodels, trying to mimic their hand and facial gestures. He was a bit bulky for a drag queen and after a few drinks his wig would begin to shift and his whiskers would start plucking through his makeup.

"What time's your performance tonight, Tony?" I pretended to be interested.

"One A.M.," he said. "Should I put you on the guest list?"

"Since when do you need to be on the guest list to get into the Wild West?" I laughed.

He pretended not to hear me, then called upstairs, "Robert, darling, are you ready?" Tony stood and leaned toward the banister, listening for Robert's footsteps, then turned toward me.

"Guess who dropped in for tea while you were away?" Tony glanced at his painted fingernails, waiting for my answer. I shrugged my shoulders.

"Your old flame, excuse the pun." He looked again for Robert. "She flew back with that other little breeder you waste so much time on, I forget her name . . ."

"Jennifer," I said.

"Oh yes, Jen-ni-fer," he said, accenting each syllable and shuddering with terror. "Robert!" he yelled.

"Was there any mail? Any phone messages?"

"The unemployment office called. They won't accept Super-8 filmmaker or four-track recording engineer as job qualifications. I tried explaining these were cutting-edge fields, but she wouldn't listen. She said if you want to be on the cutting edge, get a lawnmower." He patted my shoulder as if he agreed with her advice.

Robert came downstairs wearing a black linen suit with a white ascot, a white carnation pinned to his lapel. He had slicked back his hair and put a little rouge on his cheeks. "Bye-bye love," he said, Tony following him out the door.

I stashed the weed in an old paint can, set it on the closet floor, buried it in shoes, then took a shower and changed clothes. My body still felt in motion, the rumbling sound of Mary's car and the thought of Courtney wandering the streets, with Jennifer no less, worked itself into a glorious headache.

The remote control on the television was broken and the refrigerator was empty, so I swallowed some aspirin, grabbed my skateboard, and headed downtown for something to eat. Water gushed down the pavement, a gust of wind tried to rip the umbrella out of my hand, and I thought that any moment I might do a Mary Poppins.

Moby Dick was playing at the Jefferson Theater, the Laundromat was closed, the Plaid Pantry busy with late-night six-pack mania. The park blocks were empty, only I was stupid enough to be outside, me and the statues. By the time I reached the go-go bar, I was completely soaked.

Spider was working behind the bar. She recognized me, slipped me a beer on the house. Mary was topless, shaking her ass to the disco music. It gave me the creeps to see her up there, like a ghost under the black light, peeling off her white hot pants. I turned and faced the three fish tanks bubbling against the back wall. Nothing exotic, just some goldfish circling in dirty water.

"What's the matter?" Spider asked. "You look sad."

"Tired."

"Mary told me she had a good time." She winked, walked away to serve another customer.

I looked back at Mary in her white go-go boots and G-string, touching her toes, shaking her ass in some fat-head's face. The man slid a dollar into her garter belt, she blew him a kiss, danced out of his reach, whirled around to another drooler at the opposite side of the stage. When the song ended, Mary pulled up her shorts and came over to the bar.

"You're a sight for sore eyes," she said.

"Look who's talking." I leaned toward her, smelled her violet perfume.

"No touchy." She backed away. "Not in here, it's against the law. If you kissed me, it would be prostitution, how do you like that?"

I didn't.

"Why don't you quit this place?"

"Are you crazy?" She looked over at Spider, lit a cigarette. "I like dancing naked, it helps me understand men, and it pays a hell of a lot better than waitressing. You pigs leer either way. At least here I'm the master of ceremonies, in a restaurant I'd be a slave girl."

I lit a cigarette and stared at her lacy white bra. There was something very disturbing about Mary parading around

in her underwear. As if this were an extension of her bedroom and all these men were her lovers.

"Guess what?"

"What?"

"Spider and I rented a space opposite the Heroin Bar,
the old welfare hotel. We're going to open our own club!"

I glanced at Spider. "Don't you need a license or
something?"

"Nah, it's gonna be underground. Nobody can bust you
for having a party," she said, looking at Spider, "as long as
you don't advertise."

"How will anybody know about the place?"

She made a face like I was stupid. "We'll advertise," she
said, shaking her hips. "I have to get back to work, that new
bitch is hitting on all my regulars." She looked back at the
stage. "I'll see you later." She kissed me on the cheek. "I
miss you," she whispered, turned, and walked backstage. I
looked around at the sheepish faces of older men slouching
at their tables, sipping warm beers, the sad blonde on stage
going through the motions. It was so bleak I had to leave.

Outside the rain had stopped, but the street was still
wet. I skated around the corner to the entrance of Mary's
new space. The windows were dark, a small pile of flyers
lay scattered behind the steel gate. An old purple-faced
Indian walked up to me, asked me for change. I gave him
a quarter.

"A man froze to death here last winter." He pointed to
the spot behind the gate, his thick hands shaking. "The
ambulance drivers had to use a pickax to get him out."

I gave him another quarter hoping to dispel the curse

he'd already cast upon me. He wheeled his shopping cart down the rain-soaked street toward the Thunderbird Motel. I headed over to Hung Far Low's. The Chinese grocery next-door had a plastic horse in the window detailed with acupuncture points, behind it were glass containers with huge ginseng roots floating in blue water.

Clacking up the tiled stairs to the second floor, I went through the Chinese restaurant filled with heads bent over bowls of steaming noodles and entered the dark and smokey bar. I tried to turn as soon as I saw Courtney and Jennifer rising from their bar stools, but Courtney had already spotted me. I wasn't sure if I should hug her or choke her. She had returned to Portland with the speed of a boomerang. New York must have been more complicated than expected, although she'd have a rosy interpretation. Courtney could live under a bridge and justify it in her mind. This wasn't the first time she'd disappeared and reappeared, it was becoming a nasty habit. She loved to throw herself into situations, usually a floor or a couch in Seattle or San Francisco, accepting the forgotten invitation of a musician passing through town.

"Hey Jennifer, how was New York?" I asked.

"Fuck you!" she said and walked past me into the ladies' room.

"What's eating her?" I asked Courtney.

"Long story," she said. "So what's new with you, long time no see."

"Yeah, I guess."

Courtney corrected her posture, took a deep breath.

"Surprised to see me?" she asked, lighting a cigarette.

"Not really," I said, reached for my cigarettes, lit one too.

"Did you get my letter? I sent you a letter," she said.

I shook my head, took a drag off the cigarette, uncomfortable being alone with Courtney. She looked prettier than I remembered, humbled maybe, but for the better. Her head hung down, her tangled blond hair covering her eyes, she was staring at her shoes, asking forgiveness before I even accused her of anything. Even when she was quiet, her face was always telling you something. Her eyes had the urgency of lightning.

"Too bad," she said, "it was a good letter."

Courtney knew me like a sister. She nursed my hangovers, weaned me through all my petty depressions, helped me lie during long strained phone calls with my father. Despite all her craziness, I knew she cared a lot about me, that we worried about each other. The night before the house burned down, something was bothering her. She stayed up all night reading and writing, chain-smoking cigarettes, then slept throughout the following day. I got up and went to her room, asked about her mom. She laughed it off, said it gave her something to look forward too. But I knew it worried her, she was addicted to horoscopes and always visited a fortune-teller in Southwest Portland. Earlier that day, she had come home shaken, her eyes red from crying. When I asked what was the matter, she said that if I didn't know then there was no use talking about it, and slammed her bedroom door. A half hour later she came into my room, sat on the bed, and went into a rambling story about how she once chopped off the head of her doll with the power window of her parents' car.

"You been OK?" she asked.

"I've been OK." I shrugged. "Just went down and saw Phil."

"How's he doin'?"

"He's good. He asked about you."

"I kinda left you all wondering, huh?"

I wasn't sure what to say, opted for the silent treatment, looked away from her, scratched the back of my head.

"You don't hate me, do you?" she asked.

I tried to avoid her big blue eyes, but she leaned around looking for the slightest indication. I didn't say anything. I couldn't.

"Thank you." She hugged me.

"For what?"

"For not hating me."

I had a lot of feelings about Courtney, but our past seemed as distant now as a previous life.

"I hear you're still single." She smiled, looked up at me, tugged her choppy bangs.

"Kinda."

"Sorta maybe?" she asked.

"Actually," I said, "I'm kind of seeing someone."

"Just one? David, that's not your style."

"Her name is Mary. I don't think you know her," I said. "She's a dancer."

"I love ballet," she said.

"Me too."

Jennifer walked out of the bathroom, down the tiled stairs, waved good-bye.

"I'll see ya later." Courtney stepped forward quickly and kissed me on the cheek, turned, waved, then followed Jennifer outside, clacking down the tiled stairs two steps at a time.

I walked over to the bar, took a stool. Facing the glowing belly of the Buddha behind the bar, I ordered a vodka tonic from the bartender, a chubby Hawaiian man with a huge smile.

I felt guilty. But why? Courtney was the one that had burned down the house, but somehow seeing her again made it all seem different, as if the fire were somehow my fault.

"What makes a woman so powerful?" I asked. The bartender set my drink on a Rainier Beer coaster.

"The moon," he said, wiping the counter, pointing toward the ceiling. I looked up, squinted. Beyond the rice-paper red lights, the entire galaxy was painted on the ceiling. "You must monitor cycles very closely in a woman," he said. I lit a cigarette.

"May I have one?" Courtney asked. I turned and saw Courtney and Jennifer standing on either side of me, tilted the pack toward Courtney.

"And two more for later?" she asked.

"There's a machine near the powder room." I pointed.

"I don't have any quarters." She took three more, brushed beside me, taking matches from the bar.

"I'm sorry I yelled." Jennifer kissed my cheek. "OK if we sit with you?"

"We're not cramping your style?" Courtney asked, hesitating before taking a stool.

"Am I buying?" I asked.

"I have money." Jennifer opened her purse. "My treat."

"In that case, bartender, I'll have another vodka tonic." I shook the ice in my glass.

The bartender winked at me. "Already your fortune doubles," he said. "The Buddha likes you." He rubbed its glowing belly.

"What's the house specialty?" Courtney asked, two elbows on the bar.

"Big blue orgasms." The bartender smiled.

"I could use a couple of those, one for me, one for my friend." She pointed at Jennifer.

"Where'd you get the love beads?" Jennifer touched them, pulled them tight.

"Mary gave them to me," I said, not looking at her.

"Oh." She let go. "Still seeing the little stripper?"

"We're friends."

"I hope you didn't fuck her." She shivered.

"And if I did?"

"Really David, how low can you go? You must be getting real desperate." Jennifer sipped her drink. "How old is she, twelve? I hope you wore a raincoat."

"Jesus Christ, did you buy me a drink to persecute me."

"I want to start a band." Courtney changed the subject.

"Why?"

"'Cause I'm bored!"

"Rock stars are just vectors of lost teenage spirituality and inert fascist desires," I said, "merchandised by multinational vampires feeding on the vacancy of vulnerable baby-faced consumers."

"Oh God." Courtney leaned her head into the palms of her hands. "Here we go, the semiotics of rock 'n' roll."

I leaned toward her. "It's true, teenagers need a sacred leader, they need the crowds, the feeling of shared wisdom."

"Oh please," Jennifer cut in, "like maybe they just want to rock out."

"Exactly," I affirmed. She looked at me, sort of confused.

"So you're saying I have a Christ complex?" Courtney asked.

"Who doesn't?" I replied.

Courtney was so much smarter than Jennifer, she was fun to go one-on-one with. Jennifer's beauty had made her intellectually lazy, she doesn't have a need to connect with anyone's mind, she gets too much attention as it is. She was wearing a white see-through blouse, her breasts swallowed in a black lace push-up bra, I had to force myself not to stare whenever she leaned back into her stool.

"So what did you do while I was gone?" Jennifer asked.

"Went on a road trip with Mary."

"Leave town for the weekend and all hell breaks loose. I didn't think you had it in you."

"Are you jealous?" I asked.

Jennifer laughed. Courtney put her glass on the table.

"Want another one?" I asked.

"I've never had a multiple orgasm before." She laughed.

"Me neither," Jennifer said, placing her glass on the bar as well.

"Bartender." I signaled for another round, staring at the calm Buddha face. Jennifer put her hand on my thigh, pulled herself toward me.

"Did you miss me?" She swayed, sort of tipsy, sort of sexy.

"No, but I'm sure Robert did."

"Robert and I are over." She chewed on her straw.

"That's too bad." I took the straw out of my glass, took a big sip.

Her arm went over my shoulder, she pressed against me. "Let's go over to my house."

"Why?" I asked.

"I want you to see my souvenirs from New York," she said. "C'mon, I have some Russian vodka in the freezer. We'll trade manifestos over shots, it'll be so Bolshevik."

I looked at Courtney. She stared straight ahead, sipping her orgasm.

"You shut up." Jennifer pointed at Courtney.

"I didn't say anything." Courtney shrugged.

Jennifer looked at me. "Well?"

I was burnt-out and cashless, decided to walk them home, have a nightcap, and go home early to catch some z's.

"All right," I said, "I'll go."

Jennifer settled the bill while Courtney polished off their drinks. I slid off the bar stool, picked up my skateboard, went to the john, then followed them down the stairs and onto the street. It was raining again. I opened my black umbrella and the three of us crowded under it. Jennifer leaned drunk and cozy beside me, her cold hand slid under my wool sweater, then down over my ass.

I looked at her, she smiled, blushed, looked away. We walked up the hill through the bus mall, then across Pioneer Courthouse Square to Park Street, up the park blocks to Jennifer's apartment. She was pretty wasted, couldn't find her keys. Courtney found them in her jacket. We walked up the creaky carpeted stairs. Jennifer unlocked the door, pushed it open, we followed her inside. Courtney turned on a lamp and some tacky lounge music, an old Dean Martin record. I sat on the futon, Courtney beside me. Jennifer came out of the kitchen with a bottle of vodka, some raspberry juice, and three glasses. She sat on the floor, poured vodka into three shot glasses, then topped them off with juice.

"They're called Bloody Murders." She handed one to each of us.

"To a good night's sleep," Courtney said, toasting her glass. She threw it down her throat, then stood and went to the bathroom.

Jennifer sat beside me, hugged me.

"What's with all the affection?" I asked.

"While I was away, I thought about you a lot," she said, running her finger over the edge of my hairline. "I realized you're very special to me, that I can trust you. And you know what else?" Jennifer bent over and kissed me. I stopped her, made her look at me. Her glassy eyes had pupils big as saucers, obviously dusted. She kissed my ear, my neck, then again on the lips. A long passionate kiss.

When I pressed my hand against her breast, she kissed me harder. The toilet flushed and she stopped, pressed her head against my shoulder.

"The first night I got to New York I never felt so all alone. I wanted a friend, a close friend. I fell asleep listening to the car horns beeping at one another. I had a dream"— she leaned closer to my ear—"a wet dream," she whispered.

Courtney walked into the room.

"Oh brother!" she said, turning away.

Jennifer jumped up, grabbed her purse.

"Courtney, here's twenty dollars," she said, "go find a guitar player." Courtney hesitated, looked at me, then Jennifer.

"Please?" she insisted.

Courtney took the money, picked up her jacket, muttered something, and slammed the door. Jennifer peered through the peephole, making sure she was gone.

"Can I get you anything?" Jennifer walked back toward me, picked up the vodka bottle, refilled the shot glasses. She swallowed hers. I watched her head tilt back, noticed the thin strand of beads clinging to the delicate bones of her neck. I swallowed mine.

"Again," she said, reaching for my glass.

I'd never seen Jennifer act this way. She was always so frigid and weird.

"What are you high on?" I asked, wanting some for myself. Jennifer was always tight when it came to sharing her unchecked consumption of mood capsules.

"Nothing." She laughed. "You got any pot?"

"You seem different," I said.

"I am different," she said, setting down the vodka. "I went to New York, remember? You were the one who said I would come back with crazy ideas, how do you like them so far? Stand up." She pulled my arm, swaying, like a child pulling a tree limb.

"Why?"

"Stand up." She pulled me from the chair. I stood and was suddenly very drunk, the room felt warm and fuzzy.

"Well?" she said.

"Well what?"

She began unbuttoning my flannel shirt, twisting the buttons from their slots, then started on my belt.

"Wait a minute," I said, leaning away from her. "I don't know if I can do this, I thought we were gonna talk about Lenin?"

She followed my steps. "Too drunk to fuck?"

I stopped. Jennifer was taking the initiative, but I felt myself backpedaling.

"I love you, David," she said, kissing me on the lips, again on my neck, her hands clinging to my shoulder. "I always will." She slid them down my back over my ass, then her left hand reached between us and rubbed the erection in my jeans.

"Mary," I said, "I mean Jennifer."

Jennifer turned away, went over and slammed her hand against the beatbox, turning off the music. The room was dreadfully silent.

"Mary, Mary, Mary, all I fucking hear tonight is Mary! Is that what you want? A teenage stripper? A whore?"

"She's not a whore."

"Are you in love with Mary?" she asked, in a mocking tone. "You fuck her one weekend and forget everything? I've known you for years!" Her voice rose as she spun around to face me.

"I know, but I . . ."

"You know what?" she screamed, poured more vodka, this time only for herself. "I'm your best fucking friend," she said, quietly shaking, trying to sip the edge of her glass, looking through her purse, opening an orange pill bottle, swallowing one.

"I'm sorry." I went to her, wrapped my arms around her waist, and hugged her. She was wound up like a guitar string about to break.

"You mean it?"

"Yes," I said, kissing her forehead, then her lips, then again, more passionately. We started making out fiercely. I unbuttoned her shirt, pulled it over her shoulders. She un-zipped my jeans and placed her hand on my cock, stroking it with her fingertips.

I reached around her back and unlatched her little black bra, pulled it down from her arms, slid her skirt to her ankles. She had athlete's shoulders, wide and muscular, her skin smelled of lilacs.

She led me to her futon, lay down first, snuggling against the white comforter. I crawled on top of her, kissed her breasts, then made a wet trail with my tongue to her belly button. I climbed farther down the futon, spread her legs apart, knelt between her thighs, and started giving her head, watching her expressions as I licked the tender folds of her pussy. Jennifer's eyes closed, her hands clung to her breasts, her head swayed back and forth on the oversized white pillow. She was so beautiful, I got more excited looking at her. She lifted her butt and let out a series of muffled cries, like someone talking in their sleep. I slowed down and she cried out again, her breath racing, her stomach muscles tightened. I kissed her breasts, her neck and lips. She squeezed me tight, rolled me over, and got on top, took my hard-on and slid it gently into herself.

"David," she whispered, and pushed down upon me. Her eyes closed, she bent down and kissed me. My hands rested on her hip bones, slid up her back, tracing the delicate pattern of her spine. Her skin was smooth and soft, shining in the candlelight. Jennifer pressed her chest against mine, rubbed her cheek against my ear. Tiny gasps of air, then little cries fluttered from the back of her throat. I squeezed her ass and came inside.

Jennifer rolled off my chest, breathing heavily, her body winding down like after a long swim. I closed my eyes, felt her heart beating against mine.

When I awoke, Jennifer was curled around me, both of us stark naked. Courtney was sleeping in the same bed, her back to us, all of her clothes still on. A thin strip of light glowed around the window shade. I looked over at the clock, it was already noon.

"Shit, shit, shit." I peeled the sheets away, jumped up, and pulled my jeans on. Courtney and Jennifer didn't budge. I buttoned my shirt and laced my shoes, then crept out of Jennifer's apartment.

Outside the sky was eggshell white, overcast but bright.

My head felt like it had been chiseled on all night, a super-highway of trucks running ear to ear. The vodka had pickled my body, gave me fierce cotton mouth. Pasty, tired, my nose clogged, I lit a cigarette and felt a million times better.

Before I could piece my life together, the worst possible thing in the world happened: Mary's car drove by, her windshield a slate of white glare. I turned into a doorway, pressed myself against the building, wondering if she had already seen me. A sense of complete dread swept over me, I started worrying, thinking she may have just come from Robert's. The more I thought about it, the more certain it seemed. I was the world's biggest fuckup.

When Mary's car rolled out of sight, I hurried home. Robert and Tony were sitting on the front porch steps drinking coffee, playing with the neighbor's cat.

"Hey lover boy," Tony said, "where've you been all night?"

"How's Mary?" Robert asked.

"You mean Jennifer," Tony corrected him. They both giggled.

"What's that supposed to mean?" I asked.

"You make a mother proud," Tony said. "Two girls in one day."

"Maybe three," Robert said. "Did you do Courtney, too?"

"Fuck you." I walked past them, then stopped at the top of the stair. "Wait a minute, how do you guys know?"

"I saw Courtney last night." Robert smiled, petting the cat. "And Mary's already been by here this morning."

"Shit!"

"He looks like hell," Tony whispered to Robert.

"Fuck you," I said.

"You've got too much of a reputation, honey," Tony replied. "I don't think I can handle all that competition." They both laughed.

"Don't you have any feelings?" Robert slapped Tony's shoulder.

" 'Feelings'? I hated that song." They laughed again.

I let the door slam and went up to my room. A note was tacked to my door.

"Dear Asshole," it said. My heart started churning, I felt sick, my breath thickened, I ran back downstairs.

"What did you tell her?" I screamed.

"Nothing she didn't already know," Robert said, calmly staring at the street. "Women have incredible intuition."

I hurried down to Mary's new space above the Heroin Bar. The gate was open and the stairwell already swept. Spider was painting a mural near the landing. She gave me an ugly look, then turned away.

In the main room I found Mary talking with two other women. She headed toward me, made eye contact with me.

"You've got a lot of nerve," she said, walking past me. I followed her up the dusty stairs to a small unpainted room with four windows facing downtown Portland. She sniffed my chest.

"And you didn't even bother to shower!" She folded her arms over her breasts. "Smells expensive, what's her name?"

I couldn't decide whether to lie or confess and suffer the consequences. She was very upset, hurt. She turned her back to me.

"I was with Jennifer and Courtney, they just got back from New York."

"I saw Courtney at the Wild West last night, wanna try again?" Her voice got raspy.

"Well, Courtney left after a while. I was drunk, I wasn't thinking, I must have passed out." I pushed my hair away from my face, tried to look innocent.

"You were so tired you just conked out, is that it?" She threw her hands into the air, then planted them on her hips and stared.

"I don't know, shit, I didn't want this to happen." I felt myself blush, my voice got shaky, I looked away from her, paced to the window.

"Get out of here." She pointed. "You disgust me."

I tried to put my arms around Mary, but she pulled away.

"Go," she said, "I'll see you later. I don't want to see you now." She put her hands over her face. I tried to put my arms around her again, but she shrugged me off.

"Leave me alone!" She ran from the room. I left. I didn't want to, but I had to.

I walked through Northwest Portland, winding up and down side streets, stopping at a picnic table under the Thurman Street Bridge, near the edge of MacLeay Park. Tearing up leaves, kicking my heels into the loose topsoil, I looked into the sky. Dark clouds hovered beyond the tree line—more rain.

For months I couldn't get laid, just Jennifer stringing me
along. Mary rescued me from my stupidity. I knew Jennifer
didn't really love me, that what happened had just been
some slash-and-burn after her vacation. It'd be just like last
time, she'd joke about how drunk she'd gotten, pretend like
nothing had really happened. She would never make a
commitment, it would ruin all the psychodrama. What had
I done? I didn't trust Jennifer and now Mary didn't trust me.

I walked back to the house. Robert and Tony were
cleaning, each wearing white ruffled grandma aprons. Robert turned off the vacuum cleaner, wiped his brow with the
back of his hand. Tony fell onto the couch, fanned himself
with a magazine.

"Well?" Robert asked, they both stared, waiting for an
answer.

"Well what?" I said.

"What happened?" Robert sat next to Tony, put his
hands on his knees, eager for the gory details.

"What did she say?" Tony asked.

"She knows."

"We know that," they said simultaneously.

"She doesn't want to see me. She's really pissed off."

"That's understandable," Robert said, patting Tony's
knee.

"Do you love her?" Tony asked.

"It's too late for that," I said. "If she loved me, she
doesn't anymore."

"Do you love Jennifer?" Robert asked.

"I guess. I don't know. I don't think Jennifer's capable of love."

"What about Courtney?" Robert asked. "She's the one you really bruised last night."

"I don't want Courtney, I mean, I like her, but, fuck, she burned down my goddamned house!" I sat on the floor, took a deep breath.

"Because she loves you," Robert said.

"She's dangerous!"

"All love is dangerous."

"It's too weird. She knows me. We're too intimate, too . . ." I tried to find the word.

"Similar?" Robert cut in.

I stared across the room, focusing on the patterns in the carpeting, thinking about Mary, the ambitious exhibitionist, then Jennifer, the valley of the dolls, then Courtney, the romantic arsonist.

Robert patted my back. "You better get some rest."

"Did anyone call for me?" I asked. Robert shook his head. "Any mail?"

Robert turned on the vacuum cleaner, Tony went on dusting. I went upstairs and took a shower, lay down on my bed, and fell asleep. When I woke, the sun was already down, Robert's music thumping downstairs, Tony's electric shaver buzzing in the bathroom. I walked down the hallway, the apartment smelled like ammonia. The carpet had been sucked clean, even the slots between the banisters were dusted, the place had finally gotten the big rag it needed. The new Sonic Youth single was on, Kim Gordon's voice billowing up the stairs. I went down and saw Robert leaning over his 1200s, cueing up a record, one hand on the mixer, the other holding headphones to his ear.

"What gives?" I asked.

"I'm practicing for a straight crowd. Mary called a couple of hours ago, she stole me away from the Wild West. Double salary, that girl's got class," he said, mixing into T. Rex. He set his headphones down, put a twelve-inch back in its sleeve.

"I need some help getting this stuff down there," Robert said. "Will you give me a hand?"

"What, no groupies?" I asked.

"Getting everything home will be no problem, thank you."

"I don't know, I don't really want to see Mary."

"Don't worry about her," he said. "I fixed that over the phone when she called. We had a long talk, I explained everything." He started putting records into a plastic milk crate.

"What do you mean?"

"I told her it wasn't your fault, that once Jennifer found out you had found someone else, she stepped back in to fuck it all up so that she wouldn't lose you. It's a classic move," he said. "Christ, she might even think fucking you would make me jealous. Who knows what goes on in that girl's head." He handed me a milk crate. "What a sticky little web you've crawled into."

I didn't respond, wondered if Jennifer was that manipulative.

"You think Jennifer only slept with me to keep me from going out with Mary?"

"Wake up and smell the sidewalk."

I carried the crate out to Robert's old Cadillac, he followed with another.

"When you gonna give up women and find real devotion?" He opened the trunk.

I set the record crate in the trunk, didn't respond.

Robert was wearing white jeans, a wide blue suede belt, and a candy-striped shirt. I realized I had to change my clothes.

"Give me a second," I said. "I have to change."

"Ain't that the truth," he shot back in his campiest voice. "Mary mentioned you don't take enough showers."

Tony walked through the doorway. "Did someone say showers?" He fluttered his eyes, touched his heart.

"Do you ever give up?" I asked.

"Every chance I get, honey," he said. They both laughed. I ran up the stairs, put on some clean jeans and a new white shirt, still fresh from the Goodwill.

"David! We have to go!" Robert yelled.

I put on some deodorant, splashed a little of Tony's aftershave on my neck, then jumped down the stairs. The car was all packed up, Robert was smoking a cigarette, leaning against the trunk.

"Ready," I said.

Robert and I got into the car. He cracked the power windows, pushed in the tape, and blasted "Boogie Oogie Oogie" by Taste of Honey. We sped up Jefferson Street and into the West Hills.

"Where are we going?" I asked.

"I have to pick up some X, you want any?" Robert adjusted the rearview mirror.

The car's huge dashboard looked like a spaceship's control panel, the windshield had a strange bevel at the top. The black fins sliced through the wind as we wove up the long winding hills.

Robert's hair looked perfect, he was groomed like an extra in a fifties teen slasher flick. I was my usual sloppy self, except for the new shirt.

"Your aftershave is in competition with my car deodorizer." Robert cracked his window a little farther. "Christ, you smell like Tony." He held his nose. I cracked up.

The houses were covered from view by large evergreens and rhododendron bushes, creepy in their reclusiveness, so unlike the flat suburbs where houses are built to be seen. Stairwells had been cut into the hillsides, presumably at a time when people actually walked. Nobody uses them anymore, they're a promenade for flashers, a place for old queens to secretly meet their lovers. The first time a gay man ever came on to me was in the woods. Fag sex seems so impersonal—there's no chance of babies, so there's no anxiety. Maybe AIDS will inevitably stabilize the gay community, couples will become monogamous, adopt children, start traditional families. I looked over at Robert matting down his eyebrows with a wet fingertip, gazing at himself in the rearview mirror, and realized I was dead wrong.

We stopped in front of an A-frame house on the east side of the road. Robert shut down the car, then we walked to the door. The yard was unkempt, tall grass mixed with wildflowers, pink sweet pea, moonflowers, purple thistle, and wild daisies. We looked in the window, the house was dark. Two small candles were flickering on a coffee table near the fireplace. Music was cranking—*The Doors Greatest Hits*. Robert rang the doorbell.

"Looks satanic," he said.

Sheila opened the door. "Hi guys."

Lisa came out of the bedroom buttoning up her shirt, staring at Robert.

"Hope we didn't interrupt anything," Robert said to Lisa.

"In fact you're just in time, discomeister, I'm all warmed up." She curled around the leather sofa and laid her head on a black pillow. Sheila's film equipment was packed up in the center of the living room. The art on the wall was abstract splatterpunk, one-dimensional images that resembled squashed rats. Sheila turned down the stereo. I stood by the window staring at the skyline glowing with orange streetlight. Cities were once lit blue, and before that white, I wondered what color they would be in the future.

Sheila opened a Baggie full of little white capsules and poured them onto the glass coffee table.

"How many?" she asked.

"I'll take ten." Robert handed her a Franklin. He scooped up the capsules and placed them in the front pocket of his shirt.

"You want a beer?" Sheila asked.

"No, we have to split," he said. "I'm already late, you're both coming, right?"

"We have been for hours," Lisa said, her face pressed against the pillow, stoned out of her mind. "You don't know what you're missing."

"I know what you're missing." Robert stood up. Sheila laughed, followed us out.

"Don't take all of them at once," she said in her motherly way, and closed the door behind us.

Back in the car, Robert lit a cigarette and swerved down the hills, the road looping and changing directions like an old woman's signature. He turned left on Burnside and rolled into the city, green lights all the way into Old Town. The Heroin Bar was packed, traffic in and out was steady. We took turns carrying the equipment up the stairs. Robert gave me two capsules.

"Those are on me," he said, and winked, "in case you get stuck in an elevator."

The walls were covered with aluminum foil, the floor was painted black. Purple and red Christmas lights were draped over the windows, a black and white headshot of Sharon Tate was projected on the wall behind the stage. A small runway extended into the center of the room. Mary came out of the little door on one side of the stage and walked over to Robert. He kissed her on both cheeks. She was wearing black leather hot pants, a sleeveless black turtleneck, and black suede go-go boots. He pointed me out to her and she walked over.

"What are you doing here?" she asked.

"I came to apologize," I said.

"For what?"

"For lying."

"You mean cheating. Why should I forgive you?" she asked.

I didn't reply.

"Who are you going to sleep with tonight?" she asked.

"I'd like to sleep with you," I said.

"And the time after that?"

"You."

"Good luck." She walked away.

I walked over to Robert.

"I thought you fixed everything," I said.

"You broke it, sweetie," he said. "Don't blame me." Robert cued up a record and switched the mixer: "Love City" by Sly and the Family Stone. Robert turned his back and shuffled through the records in his crate. He put another record on the other turntable and started mixing break beats under Sly.

The stage lights were tested, then turned off altogether. Robert mixed into Alice Cooper, then Iggy Pop, working his old glam collection. A crowd had gathered at the foot of the stage, the stairwell was jammed, the doorman couldn't let people in fast enough. Cover charge was raised from three to five dollars. The art fags were coming out of the woodwork, people I hadn't seen in ages. The crowd mix was very original, polyester queens from the Wild West shoulder to shoulder with the flannel shirt syndicate of the UFO.

Within an hour the main room was packed and the upstairs bedrooms had been divided by cliques. Tony made a dramatic entrance, passed by pretending not to notice me, making a beeline for the dj booth. He was wearing a long brown wig, dressed like—what else?—a supermodel, melting through the crowd in full effect, acting ginger in high heels, rubbing his fake tits against the blushing cheeks of long-haired teenagers.

Sheila and Lisa arrived handcuffed to one another by

the belt loops of their leather pants. Lisa had obviously done every man in town and was now working her way through the women. When she saw me, she turned away, put her arm around Sheila's waist. Sheila was wearing a black leather motorcycle cap, her hair greased back, a pack of cigarettes rolled up in the sleeve of her white Harley Davidson T-shirt. They both disappeared backstage.

Courtney and Jennifer were oddly not present. I started thinking about what Robert had said, cruised the crowd, headed toward the stage. Along the right side of the dj booth, I found a windowsill to lean against and pressed my face onto the cool glass, sucking in the fresh air blowing through the gaps in the windowpane. The room was packed, people were getting restless. The lights suddenly went out and the crowd pressed forward, I sat up and peered between heads.

A big pattern of swirling psychedelic light flashed in the background, two flash pots exploded on either side of the stage, filling it with smoke. "Revolution" by the Beatles started blasting from the speakers.

The first model wore a brown leather vest with Indian beads in her hair, no bra, and matching leather hot pants. She was barefoot, ANOREXIC was written on her arm in black Magic Marker. Her hair was parted in the middle, brushed, but dirty. The clothes, too, looked unwashed, wrinkled, slept-in even, a morning after with the Manson girls. The model worked the stage like the girls at the go-go bar, as if, even with the little clothes she had on, she couldn't wait to get out of them. The second model was jailbait—fourteen, tops—wearing a sheer white puffy-sleeved minidress that

billowed like a parachute over her slender thighs. Again, no
bra and barefoot, a small wildflower tattoo above her silver
skull ankle bracelet. She acted awkward, scratched her
knee, sort of annoyed by it all, then turned and walked
offstage.

All the lights went off, "Helter Skelter" blasted from the
P.A. system. Two figures wearing black bondage gear and
carrying burning candelabras walked to opposite sides of
the stage. A strobe light came on and two naked boys ran
down the runway and stagedived into the crowd. A motorcycle roared onto the stage, a shirtless muscle-head in
leather shorts and boots was driving, a naked girl clung to
his waist, a long blonde wig cascading down her back. She
was blowing kisses to the crowd, he sneered, revving the
engine. A squadron of barefoot models, one dressed in
biker leathers, the next in a stitched suede pants suit, and
another in a cap-sleeve Soul Train T-shirt over frayed bell-
bottoms walked front and back, stomping, slouching,
graceless as possible. The last one blew a big purple bubble
of gum that splattered and stuck to her face, then picked it
off in front of the crowd and put it back into her mouth. One
girl in a denim miniskirt and purple go-go boots was topless, a silver crucifix dangled over her belly, reflecting
strobe light. She spit into the audience. The crowd cheered,
they loved it.

The girls pulled the blonde off the back of the motorcycle and carried her above their heads down the runway as
if to throw her into the crowd. A slide of Charles Manson
was projected on the back wall. Robert mixed creepy
screams into the music.

Spider was towed on stage by Sheila and Lisa, who were collared like wild slaves, Spider in dominatrix gear: shiny black plastic bra and panties, black fishnet stockings and thigh-high boots, her barefoot slaves in silver bikinis, silver eye shadow, and frosted afro wigs. Spider cracked her whip, a young skater boy in the front row screamed, flapping his hand in pain. At the far end of the runway the girls laid the naked blonde down and started laughing maniacally. The motorcycle boy revved his engine. Exhaust drifted from the stage, I started coughing, tried to open the window a tad. The models took black Magic Markers from their pockets and drew backwards swastikas on their foreheads, wrote KILL KILL on their arms and legs. The lights suddenly went off and the music stopped, the motorcycle's engine was cut. Then a recording of a wolf's cry echoed through the room, I felt goose bumps rising off my back.

"Charlie, Charlie, Charlie," the wildflower girl chanted, the other models repeating after her as they ran from the stage, the naked blonde stood and followed them, then Sheila and Lisa stood, unleashed themselves, and walked offstage. Spider cracked her whip, then climbed onto the back of the motorcycle, tweaked the pierced nipples of the motorcycle boy, licked the sweat from his back, and waved to the hysterical crowd as they rode offstage.

Mary came out and bowed, people threw roses onto the runway. She gathered them into a bunch and smiled, threw a kiss to the audience, turned, and walked offstage. I tried to catch Mary's eye, but she never looked at me. Robert mixed into techno and the lights came on, the crowd loosened. I opened the window a little farther, lit a cigarette.

When the crowd thinned out I tried to get backstage, but the hallway was packed. Jennifer and Courtney were just coming up the stairs, complaining about not being on the guest list. Jennifer was wearing a Boy Scout uniform, the shorts shortened and the top tied up over her belly button, white kneesocks showing off her tan legs. She saw me and waved, walked over, and kissed me, passionately, pressing her tongue into my mouth.

"Where'd you run off to this morning?" she asked, brushing up beside me. Courtney stood beside her casing the crowd, wearing blue jeans and a Green River T-shirt.

"Oh hi, Mary." Jennifer peered over my shoulder. "When does the show start?" I turned and saw Mary glaring.

"Smells familiar," she said coldly, then grabbed my jacket. "You're a real jerk, you know that?" Mary turned and walked away.

"Wait here," I said, looking back at Jennifer, "I'll be right back."

"Yeah, well I probably won't be here," she replied. I stopped, turned, and went back to her.

"Don't make this more difficult than it is," I pleaded.

"It's your decision." She acted annoyed.

I turned and chased Mary upstairs. Just then, the police were coming down the stairs, undercover blue shirts with radios and wallet badges.

"There's a helicopter on the roof," someone yelled.

Two cops grabbed me, pushed me up against a wall, asked me if I knew where the Manson girls were hiding. I shrugged and they pushed me onto the stairs, my head banging against the banister, my lip started bleeding. Another cop came racing down the stairs and stepped on my hand. Everyone was scrambling, trying to avoid the bust going down.

I couldn't find Mary, so I went back downstairs to find Jennifer. Two cops were arguing with people at the bottom of the stairs over some legal jargon. They didn't have a warrant, so they couldn't bust anyone. It was a private party and they were entering illegally. Mary was right, but the party was over. I went to see if Robert was inviting people over to his house.

The music had been turned off, Jennifer was in the dj booth with Robert, leaning against him, trying to squeeze between his two arms. He leaned away from her, laughing, shaking his head, trying to put records in a milk crate.

I turned away, went to look for Mary backstage.

"She just left." Spider laughed coldly.

I went to the front window and saw her car pulling away from the curb.

"Mary!" I yelled. The window slipped and banged my head. "Fuck!" I turned and saw Jennifer stretching over Robert's back, her arms around his neck, Robert trying to shimmy away.

I went back upstairs and pushed open the steel door to the roof. Twisted antennas were strapped to the chimney, black electrical tape peeling away from the pole. The air smelled like burning rubber, a few seagulls hovered overhead. The bank building was lit up, I could see cleaning people emptying wastebaskets in the oversized windows, a faint industrial orange glowing between the buildings.

Courtney was sitting on the ledge, her feet on the fire

escape, looking down onto the street. She heard me come out of the stairwell, swirled around to face me.

"Hey kissy boy," she said, "you got a light?"

"Since when do you buy cigarettes?" I handed her some matches.

"I found them," she said. "Some cop must of dropped them, there's Five-O all over the place." She pointed. I looked over the ledge, police cars were double-parked in front of the building. Courtney lit a cigarette off hers, handed it to me.

"Are you thinking about jumping?" I asked.

"No, why, you?"

I looked over the ledge again.

"Cool," she said and made room for me.

"Business as usual at the Heroin Bar, I see."

"The cops probably run that joint," she said, blowing smoke rings toward the stars.

"Are you gonna jump or what?" She acted like I was stalling or something. "I hope you're not gonna bore me with some long schmaltzy story."

"I'm still thinking about it," I said.

"Well, don't think too long, I'm not gonna sit out here all night. After this cigarette, I'm outta here."

The crowd from the party was spilling onto the street, filtering off in various directions. The West Hills were dark, the connecting dots of streetlights looping through the trees.

"Must be a slow night," Courtney said, "I think every cop in town is here, feel like robbing a bank?" she asked, raising her eyebrows, taking a hit off her cigarette.

"Not tonight."

"Where's Jennifer?"

"Downstairs, helping Robert."

Courtney shrugged her shoulders, took another hit off her cigarette.

"I saw Mary drive off with some skater boy. I thought she was your girlfriend?"

"Was."

"Is that why you came up here to jump?" Courtney flicked her cigarette butt down onto a police car.

"I hate this town," I said.

"There's worse."

"Did you come back to stay?"

"Maybe, depends on whether I can get a job."

"That's easy, you reek of personality."

"Those skills get you shitty jobs, I want a real job."

"What's a real job?" I asked.

"One that has a future."

"Of what? More work?"

"I don't want to end up in a photo booth in the middle of a shopping mall parking lot, OK?"

"I always thought that would be a cool job, looking through all those creepy photographs."

"I don't have the imagination you have." She tugged her hair, looked up into the West Hills. "I just want people to know I'm alive."

"I know you're alive."

"Not you, stupid, everyone." She stood on the ledge like some badass dictator, waving her hands at the people below. She was such a performer. If Courtney were a virgin standing on the lip of a volcano, she would do a double back flip.

"Maybe you should go back to school, you always wanted to be a writer. You love filling journals."

"How can you be a writer if you don't have a life?"

"But you have a life!" I said.

"Where?" She looked around the rooftop, picked up an empty quart of beer from the tar-paper roof, looked over the ledge. "What's better, write a novel or throw this bottle at one of those cop cars down there?" She waited for me to answer, got cocky, bouncing the bottle on her thigh.

"Depends on what you mean." I shrugged my shoulders.

"There's an old Bible saying, action speaks louder than words." She smiled like the devil and whipped the bottle, spinning it end over end toward the street. The glass shattered, the crowd dispersed, the police directed their floodlights in the direction of the rooftop. We both ducked behind the ledge, Courtney laughing in her insane way.

"Party's over," she said, jumping onto an adjoining rooftop and then another. I followed her down a rusty fire escape. We jumped, one after the other, down to a dumpster, then again down to the sidewalk.

Courtney lost her footing and stumbled onto the pavement.

"You OK?" I knelt beside her.

"I think I skinned my knee." Courtney rubbed her leg.

I gave her a hand, tried pulling her up, groaned.

"I'm not that fat!" she piped up, stood slowly, straightened her jacket, and limped through the gate. As we turned the corner, more cops drove up, followed by a fire truck and some ambulances. Sirens wailed in the distance, the droning call of reinforcements.

We crossed the street and sat on a curb between two cop cars facing the building.

"You got another cigarette?" I asked.

"There's a machine in the Heroin Bar." She pointed.

"I don't have any quarters."

Courtney handed me the pack. We smoked, watching firemen hook up their hoses to the hydrant, cops herding people off in different directions.

"Why did you go to New York?" I asked.

"Like Margaret Mead always said, there's a lot of there there."

"Why did you leave?"

"People in New York want to attach themselves to something vertical, maybe it's because of all the skyscrapers." She took a long drag off her cigarette, scooted up to the edge of the curb, wrapped her arms around her knees. "I guess I wasn't tall enough."

"Sometimes I just want to disappear, to become a gasoline station attendant at an interstate cloverleaf and wear a blue shirt with an oval patch that says DAVE." I felt a drop of rain, checked to be sure it wasn't a bird. "Have you ever thought about what you're gonna do when you get older?"

"Die," she said sardonically.

"No, I mean until then."

"Live."

"Don't you have any more plans than that?"

"No. Why? You got plans?"

"No."

"What do I look like, a fucking guru or something? You better watch it, you can't be going around asking stupid questions like that or you'll end up dancing around with a shaved head chanting Indian sutras in an airport. There's a million lost souls out there. Born Again, heard about it?"

I never thought I'd live this long, I never thought I'd get old. Courtney waved her hand in front of my face and shook her head.

"Man, you are choice. Your problem is that you're afraid of commitment. Your only example of love is your divorced parents and how shitty life was because of it." She flicked her cigarette into the street. "I know it's a big rock, but you gotta crawl out from under it." Her voice got shaky, she looked away from me, rubbed her eye with her shirtsleeve.

"What's the matter?" I put my arms around her, shook her gently. "Is it about us?" I asked. "I don't care about the fire, really, it doesn't fucking matter, I know it wasn't your fault."

"It was my fault," she sobbed.

I hugged her tight, her body was shaking.

"It was an accident, the candles. I came out of the tub and my bed was on fire. For some reason, it made me happy. I watched it burn. I didn't do anything." She looked up at me.

"It's OK, shhhh, calm down."

"What am I going to do now? I don't have anywhere to go, nobody wants me." She wiped her eyes again. "I loved you David, why didn't you love me?"

Something inside me warbled; I was her and she was

me and why had I fought this for so long? Suddenly everything seemed as obvious as air. Our lives were like two
hands clasped in prayer. I lost her once and I didn't want to
lose her again. I would do anything for her and it was up to
me to convince her.

Courtney reached for the crumpled pack of cigarettes,
lit another one, watching Mary's party slowly dissolve. Spider and another stripper walked hand in hand into China-
town. Lisa started her motorcycle, Sheila threw her leg over
the back, scooted up closer. They roared onto Burnside,
leaning around the curve. Three guys in flannel shirts went
into the Heroin Bar. I saw Tony giving directions to our
house to a group of high school boys. When he turned, they
sauntered away sheepishly toward the bus mall.

I reached over and took Courtney's hand, pressed my
fingers between hers, gave her a long stare and then a little
kiss.

"You know I love you," I said.

"Yeah right," she replied, not even looking at me.

We lay back onto the sidewalk, drizzle descending from
the pink overcast sky. I wondered what it was like to be a
raindrop, the pavement getting closer every second, tried to
catch one in my mouth. The stars seemed like the souls of
angels, the clouds like spirits from Hell, the sidewalk
smelled faintly of warm piss.

A cop kicked me.

"C'mon, assholes, move it!" he said.